PRAISE FOR *THE BOY AND THE SPY*

'It's sure to be a hit amongst those who love
edge of the seat drama and junior heroes . . .'
Magpies

'A thrilling Second World War adventure . . . this
latest book heralds a new writing path for Felice.'
Fraser Coast Chronicle

'A rollicking read, with a great setting
and action aplenty. The tension is maintained
throughout and the ending is very satisfying . . .
accessible history for kids told via a
fabulous tale. Highly recommended.'
Children's Books Daily

'All the makings of a classic children's book!'
Book of the Month, Lamont Books

This book is dedicated to Holly Smith-Dinbergs
for her on-going support, encouragement
and friendship over many years –
and for her love of the French language

PUFFIN BOOKS

FEARLESS FREDERIC

Felice Arena is one of Australia's best-loved
children's writers. He is the author and creator of
many popular and award-winning children's books
for all ages, including the acclaimed historical
adventure *The Boy and the Spy*, the bestselling
Specky Magee books and the popular Andy Roid
and Sporty Kids series.

FEARLESS FREDERIC

FELICE ARENA

PUFFIN BOOKS

PUFFIN BOOKS

UK | USA | Canada | Ireland | Australia
India | New Zealand | South Africa | China

Penguin Books is part of the Penguin Random House group of companies
whose addresses can be found at global.penguinrandomhouse.com.

Penguin
Random House
Australia

First published by Penguin Random House Australia Pty Ltd, 2018

13 5 7 9 10 8 6 4 2

Text copyright © Red Wolf Entertainment Pty Ltd, 2018

The moral right of the author has been asserted.

Design by Tony Palmer © Penguin Random House Australia Pty Ltd
Colour separation by Splitting Image Colour Studio, Clayton, Victoria
Printed and bound in Australia by Griffin Press, an accredited ISO AS/NZS 14001
Environmental Management Systems printer

A catalogue record for this
book is available from the
National Library of Australia

ISBN: 978 0 14 378675 7 (paperback)

penguin.com.au

MIX
Paper from
responsible sources
FSC® C009448

salle de boxe
THE BOXING HALL

The boy lets loose with a high kick.

But his opponent easily blocks it with the palm of his hand.

'Again!' the man shouts.

The boy repeats the kick – a strong, high piston-action with his right leg.

But the man's hand shoots out to stop his foot once more.

Then the man rushes forward, his fists high. The boy throws up his hands, but the man ducks and leads with a left-right combination punch.

The boy steps back, but he's not fast enough . . .

And the fist stops, just before it hits his torso.

The man laughs and playfully jabs his fist into the boy's stomach.

'Let me catch my breath,' the boy puffs, stepping back and shaking out his legs.

'You won't have time to rest in a real fight,' the man says. 'And that punch would have finished you.'

'But, Papa!'

'No buts, Frederic. Again! But this time lean back a little more.'

In a quiet corner of a *salle de boxe*, a boxing hall, Frederic does as he is told and charges at his father with a *chasse* frontal kick, followed by a direct *bras avant* jab.

The boxing hall is vast and spacious, bigger than any other room Frederic has ever been in and just as imposing as any grand hotel lobby in Paris.

Dusky light streams in from the ceiling-high windows onto the patterned wooden floors below. Tiny dust particles float in the shafts of light.

The hall is busy. Thirty big shirtless men are fighting one another in pairs.

The sounds of their grunting, heaving and puffing fill the space as they kick, lunge and punch. With each offensive strike, their broad shoulders and back muscles contract.

Frederic looks at them with envy. And then looks

down at his skinny legs. Perhaps one day he will be as strong as they are.

At the back of the hall, some fighters are using canes, and the crack of the sticks making contact echoes loudly.

A booming voice cuts through the noise. '*Ça va*, Claude!'

It's Monsieur Dupuis walking towards them. He is head coach at the boxing hall. He's short and stocky, and his nose sits crookedly on his face, as if it's been broken a few times in his lifetime.

It probably has, thinks Frederic.

Monsieur Dupuis twirls his bushy moustache. '*Ça va*, Frederic? Look how much you've grown. How old are you now?'

'I'll be thirteen tomorrow,' says Frederic proudly.

'Tomorrow?' cries Monsieur Dupuis. 'Then a *bon anniversaire* to you, young man. You're almost old enough to start competing. I'm happy your papa has finally brought you along with him today. He's told me all about your powerful left hook. Says he's taught you everything he knows and that you're a *boxe-française* champion in the making.

'Really?' Frederic says, surprised. He knows he has improved in the martial-arts sport of *savate*, but looking around at all the masters in the room his efforts seem small. Besides, boxing is more his father's dream than his.

'I don't know about that . . .' Frederic says.

'Of course he knows! He's just being modest,' his father boasts. 'Frederic will be a fighting hero. We've just been running through some of his kicks. He has more flexibility and power than I had at his age.'

Frederic blushes. He looks up to see his father beaming proudly at him. He tries to mirror his smile, but only manages a half grin.

'Magnificent,' says Monsieur Dupuis. 'Well, when Frederic is ready to take it to the next level, perhaps he could train with my newest champion.'

Monsieur Dupuis turns and calls out, 'Joseph! Come and meet Monsieur Claude Lefosse and his son.'

A blond-haired young man leaves his opponent and brushes his way past the other men to join them. He looks every bit the fighter – solid and muscular.

'Claude was my prodigy many years ago, until his knees gave in,' says Monsieur Dupuis to Joseph. 'He sometimes helps out here and coaches some of the youngsters.'

Joseph nods and wipes his palms on the back of his pants before shaking Frederic's father's hand.

'Joseph is from Marseille,' Monsieur Dupuis tells

them. 'Just moved to Paris. He is going to win us the championship this year – his legs are so strong he could kick you to the moon and beyond!'

Joseph crosses his giant arms and looks at Frederic. 'How about you and I go for a round, boy?'

'Huh? What?' Frederic can't believe it. Nerves shoot through his body like lightning. He can't be serious! How can I go head to head with him? I haven't fought anyone except for my father.

But Frederic's father is smiling and nodding.

Joseph chuckles. 'I just mean a friendly bout,' he says. 'What sort of man do you think I am? I just want to see your combat style. So, Frederic, are you up for a little sparring?'

'Go for it,' says Frederic's father, gently pushing him forwards. 'Show them what you've got.'

crochet du gauche
LEFT HOOK

Frederic rolls up his sleeves and strikes a kickboxing pose: his fists raised and clenched. He tries to make his stance wide and strong.

'I'll referee,' says Monsieur Dupuis. 'Frederic, there are only four kinds of kicks and punches. No shin and knee strikes allowed. And as for the punches . . . straight blows, uppercuts and hooks are permitted.'

He turns to Joseph. 'Strictly no contact from you,' he says. 'Got it?'

They both nod.

Frederic knows he needs to use the element of surprise to have any chance of staying in the fight.

Joseph towers over Frederic – he's at least twenty

centimetres taller and looks as if he weighs twice as much.

'Fight!' Monsieur Dupuis calls out, stepping back.

Frederic lets loose with a couple of *bras avant* front-arm jabs.

Joseph stumbles backwards, caught off guard.

Frederic hears Monsieur Dupuis laugh. Some of the other fighters in the hall stop their training to watch.

Frederic keeps advancing towards Joseph and strikes out with a *fouetté* – a roundhouse kick, high to the face – and then another, low to the gut.

Again Joseph is forced to react quickly to avoid him.

Frederic hears a cheer from the fighters gathering around to watch and feels a thrill. This is what it must feel like to compete in the ring, he thinks. No wonder Papa loved boxing so much.

But immediately Joseph regains composure and blocks an incoming *coup de pied bas*, a low sweeping kick to the shin.

'Frederic!' cries Monsieur Dupuis. 'I said no shins.'

Joseph shoots off a few lead jabs – left, right, left, left, right – and Frederic dodges each one, swaying and side-stepping each incoming strike.

There are benefits to being small – he's agile and

nimble on his feet. But Joseph reads his every move. He continues to charge forward with a *coup de pied au corps*, a kick directly into Frederic's body. Frederic can't avoid it. He feels Joseph's toes tap against his stomach.

That was a strong kick, he thinks, grateful there's no contact.

'You have some fancy moves there, boy,' Joseph says, shuffling from foot to foot. 'But remember looking good and dodging my fists is one thing, but it takes an actual strike to win. So don't hold back. I'm a big guy, I can take it.'

He advances again, stepping in with another right jab. Frederic ducks and immediately rockets upward. And as he is about to release a *crochet du gauche* – a left hook – to Joseph's face, he pulls away his punch at the last second.

The hall erupts again. The other fighters all know that was a perfect opportunity to knock the champion off his feet.

Even Joseph appears to be impressed.

In a competition fight, Frederic would've won some major points had he followed through with such a well-executed blow.

Monsieur Dupuis rushes in between them, hands in the air.

'That's it!' he shouts. 'Give it up for Frederic!'

Frederic glances over to his father, looking for his proud smile. He is proud of himself.

This time I've earned it, he thinks.

But to his confusion his father looks disappointed.

Joseph steps up to Frederic, ruffles his hair and then shakes his father's hand.

'You've taught him well. Flawless skills,' Joseph says to Claude. 'But there's more to be done. You'll have to draw out his inner tiger . . . otherwise he'll never be competitive in the ring and he might get seriously hurt.'

Despite the praise, Frederic feels now as though he has somehow let his father down. Inner tiger? What does that mean? he wonders.

'Did you hear that?' Frederic's father tells him. 'You did well, but you've got to attack more. A boxing champion needs to be relentless and unflinching.'

Frederic nods.

'That's what you want, isn't it?' his father says. 'To be a boxing champion. That's what we both want.'

But it's not really a question, and Frederic doesn't answer him.

bon anniversaire
HAPPY BIRTHDAY

The next morning Frederic wakes to the familiar sound of hooves on the cobblestones of his street. It's a sound that has always comforted him. He smiles without opening his eyes.

The horses pass by his house. They're from the stables just a few blocks away, and they're on their way to be bathed in the Seine River. Frederic has always dreamt of working with horses and normally he would go to watch them, but not today – he has something else planned.

He hops out of bed and slips into his knee-length baggy trousers, puts on his collarless shirt and braces, and ties on his scuffed black shoes before tiptoeing out of his room. It's just a nook in the corner of the living room of his family's small ground-floor apartment, but he loves it.

Off the living room there's a small kitchen, a bathroom and his parent's bedroom – their door is open. He peeks in. It looks as though his mother is still fast asleep.

'I can hear, you know,' she says from under the bed sheet. 'Your steps are as heavy as the hooves of those carriage horses.'

'Sorry, *Maman*,' says Frederic, running into the room and jumping to sit on the bed next to her.

'Your father should be finished work soon,' she says, sitting up. 'Don't forget that you're meeting him at a different spot today – so don't be late!'

Almost every day of the summer Frederic has woken up early to meet his father on his way back from his night shift.

Claude works as a guard at Paris's most famous art museum – the Louvre. But Frederic has never before been inside. Tonight he will get a chance to go to work with his father for the first time.

'Are you excited, *mon cher*?' asks his mother, hugging him.

Frederic is buzzing with excitement but he tries to act calm.

'I guess,' he says, wriggling out of her arms. He slaps on his flat cap and pulls it down over his eyes. 'Do you know what the surprise is? Why does Papa want me to meet him somewhere else this morning?'

'My lips are sealed.' His mother grins, then leans in and kisses him on the forehead. '*Bon anniversaire*, Frederic. Thirteen! I can't believe it. It seems that only yesterday I was cradling my beautiful baby boy.'

'*Maman!*' Frederic winces.

'What? I don't care how grown up you get, you'll always be my baby boy. Now, you'd better get going, you don't want to keep your father waiting. And I better get moving too. Fashion waits for no one.'

Frederic's mother is a seamstress at one of Paris's large fashion houses. She sews and mends clothes for wealthy ladies. She's an expert in creating gowns for all occasions from morning to evening. The rich ladies even have special outfits for walking.

Frederic can't understand why anyone would need more than one outfit. But his mother has told him that the rich ladies need to be beautiful – with shoulder and waist trimmings and delicate needlework on their skirts and dresses.

When he had asked her why she didn't have trimmings too, she had said: 'The poor wear linen, the middle-class wear cotton and the rich wear silks. So

I will have to be content with linen, *mon cher*.'

'*D'accord!* Time to go,' she orders. '*Allez! Allez!* Go! Go!'

Frederic waves goodbye and steps out onto the street. The light seems more golden this morning. The narrow apartment buildings with their wrought-iron balconies filled with hanging plants and flowers seem even more beautiful than usual.

'*Bonjour!* Good day!' comes a cry from the balcony of a building opposite.

Frederic looks up to see *les grands-mères du balcon*, the balcony grannies. He doesn't know their real names, but every day he can remember they have been seated on their second-floor balcony, keeping watch on the street and greeting him as he walks to meet his father.

'Why are you looking so smug this morning?' one of the sisters calls out to Frederic.

Frederic just grins.

'Boys are always smug!' declares the other sister.

'But he has a spring in his step today!'

'What's he up to? What are you up to, boy?'

'He doesn't say much!'

'He never says much!'

Frederic waves cheekily to them, turns right and keeps moving.

He picks up his pace, walking past the vendors opening their stores, café owners putting out sidewalk tables and chairs, and restaurateurs unloading food supplies from horse carts. The aroma of coffee and freshly baked bread wafts in the air and Frederic feels a pang of hunger.

Perhaps Papa and I will get something special to eat for my birthday, he thinks.

'Vive la France! Vive la France! Vive Bleriot!' A small boy with a big voice is standing outside a café yelling at the passers-by.

It's Journal – or that's the name Frederic knows him by. It's been his nickname ever since he started selling newspapers. He's Frederic's age but has been working for years. There's nothing he doesn't know.

Journal announces the day's headlines to anyone willing to listen, anyone who might buy the paper from him.

Frederic is always ready to listen. He doesn't have money to throw away on papers but wishes he did. The stories are always incredible – amazing new discoveries, thrilling wars and battles in far off countries and jaw-dropping inventions like a contraption called a vacuum cleaner and a motion-picture camera projector invented by two French brothers.

'July 9th, 1909! Bleriot! Bleriot flies over the sea!'

Journal hollers, waving today's edition of *Le Matin*.

Frederic runs over to look. On the front page is a photograph of a man standing proudly by a flying machine. The huge headline reads: *The Great Frenchman Louis Bleriot – the First Man to Fly over the English Channel in an Aeroplane!*

'It's incredible!' Frederic says. 'It's mind-boggling. Men flying? What next?'

'Just you wait! We'll all be flying to the stars one day,' says Journal.

'No way! Do you really think so?'

'Absolutely!' says Journal.

Frederic tips his cap and breaks into a fast jog – he doesn't want to keep his father waiting.

By the time he is bolting across the plaza in front of the *Hôtel de Ville*, Paris's impressive town hall, he is puffed, but he wants to pass his favourite statue on the way so he runs harder and takes the long way round.

He darts past a group of people, poorly dressed and huddled together like pigeons. A few of them are sitting on old wooden fruit crates. One of them, a young woman, jumps out in front of Frederic and startles him.

'Got some food?' she says, putting out her hand. Her palms and face are covered in soot and grime.

There are so many homeless people in this neighbourhood, Frederic thinks. They're always begging!

He shakes his head, sidesteps the girl and continues on running.

He needs to cross at a bridge to reach the *Île de la
Cité*, a island in the Seine River, so he runs until he
reaches the *Pont d'Arcole*.

Over the bridge is the enormous, ancient Notre
Dame Cathedral but that's not why he's come.

Dashing past the cathedral, he steps up to a bronze
statue of a man on horseback. It's supposed to hon-
our the famous king and emperor Charlemagne, but
Frederic is here for the horse, not the man.

He stands alone in front of the giant bronze
statue – it's too early in the morning for crowds.
Amazingly lifelike and majestic, the horse is
powerful yet graceful at the same time. It's the type
of horse Frederic dreams of riding one day.

Frederic admires the statue for a few minutes
before turning and running towards the *Pont au
Double*, an iron-cast bridge that connects the *Île de la
Cité* with the Left Bank of the city.

'What took you so long?' Frederic's father calls
out to him, already standing in the middle of the
bridge. 'Don't tell me you're slowing down in your
old age!'

Frederic smiles as his father hugs him.

'*Bon anniversaire!*' Claude says. 'Are you ready for your birthday surprise?

l'aigle
THE EAGLE

Claude gestures for Frederic to follow. They jostle and bump into each other, shadow-boxing and laughing as they walk across the bridge and into the Left Bank of the city.

They cross a busy road, dodging horse-drawn cabs and motor cars. Even though they are now a part of everyday life, Frederic still marvels at the automobiles – their open-air carriages, large wheels and their *put-put* noisy engines. Most of them have been made by the great French motor car manufacturer De Dion Bouton.

A man with a scruffy long beard shuffles up to Frederic and his father. At first Frederic thinks it's another homeless person begging for money, but as the man gets closer he sees it's one of the many silhouette artists who make their money selling paper cut-outs to tourists in the city.

The man is holding up a paper silhouette cut-out and Frederic leans forward to look – it is an amazingly detailed cut-out of a man and a boy, in a fighting stance, their arms and legs suspended in action.

Frederic smiles. It's very impressive. He is always amazed at how quickly the men work – cutting out images as if they are drawing a sketch.

'For you,' the man says. 'It *is* you.'

'No, thanks. Not today,' says Frederic's father politely, brushing past the man.

'Sorry, I didn't hear that?' says the artist, cradling his art materials and scissors close to his chest and falling into step with Frederic's father. 'I'm a bit deaf. Did you say perhaps later today?'

'No, I didn't,' Frederic's father says, laughing. 'Sorry, Monsieur, I'm not interested. Good day to you.'

Frederic glances back over his shoulder to see the artist approaching the next people who step off the bridge.

'It was very good,' Claude says to Frederic, 'but I have something else to buy this morning.'

A few minutes later they turn into a narrow alley called *rue de la Bûcherie,* and Frederic's father leads him to a store with a sign above the door. In swirly white lettering it says: *Jouets et Articles de Paris*, Toys and Articles of Paris.

'Really?' says Frederic. 'A toy store?' He feels disappointed.

'I knew it!' exclaims Claude. 'I know you're thinking – I'm a little too old for toys! Well, we're not here for a toy.'

A small bell chimes above the door as Frederic and his father step inside.

The first thing Frederic notices is the almost overpowering scent of wood and polish.

He doesn't know where to look first. On shelves reaching from floor to ceiling are dolls, fabric bears, miniature kitchen equipment, board games, marionettes, novelty cards, and curious playthings that he has never seen before. The entire floor of the store is packed with tricycles, wicker prams, wooden sailboats and rocking horses.

'Ah, Monsieur Lefosse,' comes a gruff voice from the back of the store. 'I just opened – early for you, as arranged.'

A giant of a man steps up to them. Frederic thinks he looks more like a pig farmer or a soldier than a store-owner. His hands are the size of boat paddles, and he almost crushes Frederic's hand when he shakes it. His cheeks and large nose are flushed bright red.

'I'm Monsieur Bertrand,' he says, smiling, 'and your father has been waiting for this day for a long time now. I have your surprise at the back. Just wait.'

Frederic furrows his brow.

His father winks at him.

When Monsieur Bertrand returns, he is holding a strange-looking contraption. It's large – almost as tall as Frederic. Cotton canvas is stretched over a bamboo frame and it is shaped to look like a bird in flight. The bird's wingspan is wide and strong. Its head turned to show off a regal profile.

Frederic gasps. 'Papa! Is that what I think it is? A *cerf-volant*?'

'Yes, yes, it is! It's a kite!' His father laughs at Frederic's shock. 'I told you it wasn't a toy!'

Frederic can't believe it. Kites are rare and expensive. Owned by wealthy adults and sometimes their wealthy children. How can his father even afford such a magnificent thing?

'I know we haven't been able to give you a lot of things in the past,' his father says. 'But your mother and I decided two years ago that we'd put aside some savings each week for your thirteenth birthday.'

Frederic is beaming as Monsieur Bertrand hands the kite over to him.

'It's called *l'Aigle*, the Eagle,' he says. 'My cousin Charles designed it. He's the leading kite maker in all of France, and you, young man, are one of the very first to have it. I wish I'd had this one at the Games.'

'The games?' says Frederic. 'The Olympic Games?'

Frederic's father nods. 'Monsieur Bertrand competed in the kites event at the Summer Olympic Games here in Paris,' he says.

'That was only nine years ago. And look how far we've come in aviation since then,' Monsieur Bertrand adds proudly. 'Those Americans, the Wright brothers, getting all that attention for the first engine-powered flight. But it was us French that were the first to take to the sky – where would the world be without the Montgolfier brothers and their hot-air balloon, eh?'

'And don't forget the Frenchman who just flew over the English Channel,' says Frederic.

'Look who's up to date with the latest news!' says Monsieur Bertrand.

'We might head out of the city this Sunday to fly it,' Frederic's father says to him. 'We'll make a day of it with your mother. What do you think?'

Frederic beams and nods as he and his father say goodbye to Monsieur Bertrand.

le cheval
THE HORSE

Frederic feels as if he's the luckiest person in all of Paris to have such a gift in his hands. His mind drifts, imagining what it will be like to fly his kite, wondering how high he can make it go.

'Are you happy?' asks his father.

But before Frederic can answer, his father curses. A few metres ahead of them on the other side of the bridge, Frederic sees the silhouette artist they had met earlier. He is frantically trying to grasp at a handful of his creations that are fluttering in the wind, but the paper cut-outs are flying across the road and into the busy traffic of horses, carriages and motor cars.

At first Frederic doesn't understand what is happening, but then he watches as the man steps back and in the way of an approaching motor car.

In what feels like slow motion, the car swerves to the other side of the road towards them, forcing Frederic and his father to jump out of its way. It speeds down the road, almost colliding with another motor car.

Horns honk and people shout and at the end of the bridge a horse rears up with a terrified sound, spooked by the near miss.

The groom leading him cries out as his horse bolts and breaks away.

Pedestrians scream and scurry sideways to get out of the way of the frightened animal.

But all Frederic can think of is the horse. In such a frantic state it might slip over the cobblestones and break its leg or, worse, get hit by a motor car. He pushes the kite into his father's arms and races towards the terrified horse. He skids to a stop directly in its path.

Behind him he hears his father yell. 'No, Frederic! No!'

tel courage
SUCH COURAGE

Frederic holds his open hands in front of him. His heart is racing but his breathing is calm. He no longer hears his father calling to him. He doesn't react to the people and bikes scattering around them.

All he sees is the horse charging towards him.

Strangely Frederic isn't afraid. His feet feel as if they've been stuck to the ground.

The horse abruptly stops only a couple of metres from Frederic and rears up onto its hind legs, snorting and whinnying. Its ears are pinned back and its nostrils are flaring.

When its front hooves clatter on the cobblestones again, Frederic can see that its eyes are white and large. He can feel its panic.

'*Reste calme – shhh*, stay calm,' Frederic says in a soothing voice. He is as still as he can be. 'I'm not going to hurt you.'

The horse dances around terrifyingly close to Frederic. He knows that if it panics again it will knock him down and he will be trampled under those huge hooves. But the horse is not panicking now – it begins to settle. Its ears move forward a little and its heavy breathing slows.

'That's it,' Frederic says, inching forward. 'Nice and easy. You're okay.'

With his right palm open, Frederic slowly reaches for the muzzle. He looks up at the horse and sees for the first time how beautiful it is – a chestnut brown mare with a dark tail and mane.

The mare grunts and steps forward to sniff at Frederic's hand. He slowly raises his other hand and gently pats the side of her face.

'Thank you! Thank you!' cries the horse's groom, running up to them and taking hold of the strap. He's a spindly young man, not much older than Frederic. Frederic doesn't know him, but he has seen him before, handling the horses by the river. 'I can't believe what you just did. You're a natural. Truly. I'm Leon. My uncle runs the stables on *rue Vieille du Temple* in

Le Marais. He's always looking for extra help. If you want a job you should drop by and see us.'

Frederic nods. He is buzzing with excitement as the groom leads the mare away. He realises he is smiling crazily but he can't stop – even when his father throws his arms around him.

'I can't believe it! *Tel courage*! What were you thinking?' he says.

'I don't know,' says Frederic. 'I just did it.'

'Well, that's the courage that Joseph was talking about yesterday. You've got to show no fear and go for it. It's that type of backbone and daring that shows you have the traits of a great fighter, my son. I'm very proud of you.'

Frederic nods but his smile is fading now.

It was the horse! he thinks. Fighting doesn't make me feel like this.

And a job with horses! How magnificent would that be?

He hopes his father will understand.

Musée du Louvre
THE LOUVRE

Later that day, when the summer daylight has turned to a soft pink haze, Frederic and his father set out for the night shift.

Frederic's mother sees them out the door 'Don't get in your Papa's way,' she says.

'He won't get in the way, my love,' said Frederic's father, kissing her before they step into the street. 'See you tomorrow morning.'

The balcony grannies are perched in their usual spot, looking down at the busy street below.

'Monsieur!' cries one of them to Claude. 'Your son doesn't say much, does he?'

Frederic's father greets them, tipping his hat.

'*Bonsoir, Mesdames*, Good evening, ladies! He's more action than words, my boy!'

'Action? Action always leads to trouble!' one of the ladies retorts.

'Boys are drawn to trouble like rats to sewers. I'd keep an eye on that one if I were you,' adds the other cheerfully.

Frederic and his father laugh and wave goodbye to the balcony grannies and set out for work.

Everything about the Louvre museum is grand. When Frederic stands in front of the colossal building on the banks of the Seine River, he almost can't believe he will be allowed inside.

He wishes he had someone to tell this amazing story to. Since he finished primary school last month he hasn't seen any of his classmates. They have all found jobs and gone to work and he knows he will soon have to earn his own way in the world too.

He wasn't close to anyone in particular at school anyway. Perhaps I can tell Journal something for once, he thinks.

The museum was first a fortress and then a king's palace. Everything about it is royal and bold – especially the statues on the façade and the giant stone arch, the *Arc du Carrousel*, with its four gilded bronze horses pulling Emperor Napoleon in a chariot.

Frederic is excited as his father leads him down a narrow laneway that carves into the museum building. They walk away from the main public entrances and through a hidden doorway.

He feels as if he is joining some sort of secret society. When they step inside, they wind their way through a labyrinth of narrow corridors that lead to a small room.

Frederic holds his breath as his father opens the door . . .

Then he sighs, underwhelmed. Behind the door is a cramped change room, lined with wooden cupboards.

Nothing grand about this, Frederic thinks.

'*Bonsoir*, Claude!' says a man wearing a guard uniform.

'*Bonsoir*, Marcel,' says Frederic's father as he opens a cupboard and takes out his uniform and a truncheon.

Claude introduces Frederic to his colleague as he changes into his uniform.

'You're going to spend an evening with the greats tonight, Frederic,' says Marcel as other guards come and go. 'And I'm not just talking about me and your father!' Marcel laughs at his own joke and Frederic smiles politely.

When Frederic turns back to his father, he almost doesn't recognise him. He looks so different in uniform.

He's wearing a navy blue double-buttoned jacket over a light blue shirt. His pants are crisp and his boots are shining. His cravat and cap are neat and clean. Frederic has never seen his father looking so smart and official before.

'We're all assigned to different wings of the museum,' Claude says, 'but tonight I'm going to give you the grand tour, so I hope you're ready for a lot of walking.'

The three of them make their way through two more narrow doorways, before stepping into a large hallway.

'The Denon Wing!' Claude announces. 'Let's begin with some of the Italian greats.'

Frederic's jaw drops. He has never seen so many paintings gathered together – they line the walls of a grand corridor that seems to go on forever.

Frederic and his father say farewell to Marcel.

'You know most of the guards that work here have a background in *savate* like me,' says Frederic's father. 'Except for Marcel. Marcel comes from Le Havre, where he worked as a wharf hand. He is one of those small-town, street-tough men that would make those apache gangs around *Montmartre* quake in their dandy boots. This type of job is only given to the toughest and strongest.'

'So why did they hire you?' Frederic says cheekily. Then he quickly ducks as his father grabs him in a playful headlock.

For the next few hours Frederic shadows his father through the great hallways of the museum.

He stands for a long time in front of a painting of a horse race – the jockeys urge their horses on under a dark stormy sky, and Frederic can almost hear the thunder of hooves. He thinks of the mare in the street and her wild eyes.

His father calls him away and by the light of the lantern more paintings of great historical figures and scenes and battles seem to come to life. But after a while, as the night wears on, Frederic begins to tire. The works of art all start to look the same and the galleries and corridors seem darker and a bit spooky outside the light of the lantern.

Around midnight Frederic finds a bench, upholstered in plush red cushion, and his father leaves him to sleep.

Later, he wakes to Claude gently nudging him.

'You picked a prime spot,' he says, holding his lantern up to a small painting in front of Frederic. 'Her name is *La Joconde*, the jovial one, by an Italian artist called Leonardo Da Vinci. She's one of my favourites. But I can never tell if she's actually smiling. It depends on which angle you're looking at her from. Come stand here with me.'

Frederic steps in closer to his father and looks back at the painting.

'I think she is smiling,' he says. 'Or perhaps that's the way she looks when she's hungry.'

Claude laughs. 'I get the hint! That's why I came to get you. Time to head back to the change rooms and have something to eat.'

'On our way, could we go back to see that horse painting?'

Claude nods. 'That painting, as fine as it is, has nothing on this one. Why does that interest you so much?'

Frederic shakes his head. 'No reason,' he says.

After a break, with his stomach filled with bread and cheese, Frederic follows his father back to a salon called the *Galerie d'Apollon*. On the way there, Frederic's father suddenly freezes. He cranes his head slightly, as if he has just heard something.

'Intruders,' he whispers. 'Stay close!' And he begins to walk quickly towards the salon.

voleurs
THIEVES

As they get closer to the *Galerie d'Apollon*, Frederic hears a thumping sound, followed by muffled voices.

Handing the lantern to Frederic, Claude takes his truncheon from his belt.

Frederic's heart is racing. There's no denying he's afraid, but his father expects him to follow so he does. He takes a deep breath.

My father will keep me safe, he thinks. And he expects me to be brave.

They peer around the corner of the entrance to the chamber. Three men are in the process of removing a portrait from the wall.

They look like gangsters – wearing waistcoats,

trousers that are tight at the knees and flared at the bottom, and sailor caps. All three are wearing black eye masks.

Frederic's father takes out a whistle from his jacket pocket and blows sharply again and again.

'Don't move!' he calls, raising his truncheon. His voice echoes off the grand, gilded walls of the gallery.

Frederic's father is tough and his voice is deep and filled with authority. Frederic expects the thieves to turn and bolt.

But they don't. Instead they drop what they're doing, clench their fists and move forward.

'Marcel will be on his way,' Claude says to Frederic. He crunches his neck and stretches his shoulders backwards – Frederic knows he's preparing to fight.

But there is no sign of Marcel and Frederic begins to panic as the men move closer. His father can't take them all on.

'I'll find Marcel,' Frederic says, putting down the lantern.

'He'll be here,' says his father. 'But right now, I need you to step up with me, son. I know you can do it. Show them that courage I saw the other day on the bridge.'

Frederic raises his fists. The men are only metres away.

But in the lantern light, Frederic can see that his fists are shaking. He suddenly knows he *can't* do this. That his father needs a real fighter.

'You need Marcel, Papa!' he says. 'He'll help you.'

His father nods, and Frederic grabs the lantern and runs.

Frederic dashes into the darkness, his lantern swinging and shaking from side to side, causing shadows to dance on the wall. He runs to the eastern part of the wing, where Marcel, during their food break, had told them he would be.

'Marcel! Marcel!' he cries. 'We need help!'

But Marcel is nowhere.

This is crazy! Where is he? Frederic thinks, already turning and charging back towards his father.

Frederic gasps with every stride, his lungs burning. As he reaches the *Galerie d'Apollon*, two of the men bolt out in front of him, one of them clutching the portrait in his arms. They almost knock him over as they run past.

And just as Frederic is about to take a sharp right into the room, he collides head-on with the third thief. They both crash to the ground, the thief's mask and cap go flying.

In the flicker of the lantern's light, now spinning on the ground, Frederic gets a brief, but good, look at the man. His eyes are beady and intense and he has an unusual streak of white hair – as if someone had painted a stripe on his slicked-back black hair.

The thief springs to his feet, scoops up his cap and sprints away after the others.

Frederic's legs wobble as he regains his balance and runs into the room.

His father is lying on the floor, motionless.

'Papa!' Frederic falls to his knees at his father's side, his heart sinking to his stomach. He can't breathe. He shakes his father frantically, tears streaming down his face.

But he can't wake his father up.

la pluie
RAIN

The rain falls. And it doesn't seem as if it's ever going to stop. Every day during the first three weeks in January 1910 grey skies hang over Paris, soaking everything. But in this new year, Frederic barely notices the bleak wintry days.

It's dawn but still dark outside as he ties his boots, throws on his heavy woollen overcoat and steps towards the front door.

'Don't forget to eat something,' comes his mother's voice.

Frederic turns back to his mother's room. He sits on the edge of her bed.

'I won't, *Maman*,' he says softly. 'I'll eat something

once I get to the stables.'

There's silence. Frederic can tell what his mother is thinking. He's waiting for her to say something. But she doesn't, so he does.

'It's his birthday today,' he says in almost a whisper.

'I know, *mon cher*. He would've been forty-one.' She sighs heavily.

Frederic has become used to her sighs. They come in waves, in long breathy murmurs filled with deep sorrow and pain. He sighs the same way.

It's been almost six months since that traumatic night in the museum – the night his father died – but they are still adjusting to Claude's absence. Still expecting him to come home. His mother still occasionally sets a third place at the table. Frederic still lies in bed every Sunday wondering why his father hasn't woken him for their usual *savate* training session. Before he remembers . . .

Even though the long police investigation was over they still had not caught the thieves or recovered the painting. After all the painful questions, all they knew was that Marcel had been an insider working with the thieves.

The newspapers had focused more on the stolen portrait, than on Claude's death. Frederic had avoided walking past Journal for a long time to avoid hearing about the theft and being reminded of what happened.

At times it had all been too much to deal with.

Frederic's mind drifts. Last year, he would have been getting ready to go to school, after meeting his father on his way home. But now he has to work. The income that Frederic's mother makes as a seamstress is not enough to keep them both.

Frederic kisses his mother goodbye and heads out into the biting cold. It's grey – again – but at least the rain has eased off for now.

Frederic looks up for the balcony grannies. It's too early and too wet and cold for them, he thinks. But the balcony door abruptly swings open, and one of the grannies steps up to the railing. She is covered in furs from head to toe, as if she's about to trek the Alps.

'Another day of shovelling horse manure, boy?' she says, not unkindly.

Frederic nods. '*Oui, Madame*,' he mutters, his shoulders hunched and his hands deep in his pockets.

'Nothing keeps a boy more honest than handling an animal's poop,' she says.

Frederic shrugs and continues walking. He doesn't have far to go. First a right into *rue Sainte-*

Croix de la Bretonnerie, and then a quick left into *rue Vieille du Temple*.

Five minutes later, Frederic reaches the place that has become his life for the past couple of months – the Saint Jean Stables and *Fiacre* Depot.

Out the front, several carriages are lined up ready for hire. He walks past the front one and pats the side of the horse out front. It's *Tempête*, Storm, the mare that had been spooked by the motor car on Frederic's birthday last summer.

He runs his hand over Storm's soft nose and she snuffles at his jacket, hoping for treats.

He feels comforted for a moment but then feels overwhelmed by guilt.

Would I have this job if my father were still alive? He wanted me to train with Monsieur Dupuis. He would have done everything he could to make that happen.

Frederic is grateful for the job Leon and his uncle Gustave have given him. It's a dream come true for him working with the twenty-five horses in the stables.

Boss Gustave, as he likes to be called, is a good man, but Frederic knows he won't stand anyone being late for work.

'Sorry, Storm,' he whispers. 'I've got to go.'

'You're late!' Boss Gustave barks as Frederic push-es open the large wooden door leading into the stables. 'And I need you to do a very important errand. I've just acquired another horse from the Alma Stables, and I want you to go get it and bring it back here. But . . .' He pauses and pulls a face.

'But what?' asks Frederic.

'It's not the friendliest of beasts. He needs re-training. You can use your magic touch to settle him down.'

'Magic touch?' Frederic laughs. Leon had told Boss Gustave about what happened with Storm and he was straightway convinced that Frederic had a special way with the horses.

'Watch the traffic when you lead him back – go via the back streets if you can. And when you return, I want you to muck out *Soleil*'s, *Flocon*'s and *Rafale*'s stalls.'

Boss Gustave names all the horses in his stable after different types of weather – Sunny, Snowflake, Windy and Storm. He's obsessed with the daily forecast.

'I'm sure there's more wretched rain on its way,' he says as he leaves the stable.

Leon saunters up beside Frederic and hands him a baguette.

'*Bon appétit*, my friend. What's my uncle going on about today?' he says.

'I'm going to Alma Stables to get a horse. It's going to take me a couple of hours.' Frederic stuffs his mouth with the warm, freshly baked bread. 'It would be so much quicker if I could ride the horse back.'

'*Shhh!*' hisses Leon, almost choking on his last bite. 'If my uncle hears you even talking about riding these horses, you'll lose your job. Carriage horses are not for riding. Besides who do you think you are? A soldier?'

'Frederic?' calls Boss Gustave. 'I'm not paying you to eat and chat. Go! Now!'

onze
ELEVEN

It takes Frederic well over an hour to reach the Alma Stables. The trip is made longer by the fact that Journal stops him with the news along the way.

'The Seine's banks overflow,' he calls, waving a newspaper. 'Small towns and villages underwater! Landslides! Rising water!'

'Landslides?' Frederic repeats.

'Yes, look,' says Journal, flipping through the paper and showing Frederic an illustrator's impression of a town submerged under mud and water.

'That's unbelievable,' Frederic says. He notices that Journal has a half-eaten apple sitting on a pile of his newspapers.

'Are you going to have the rest of that?' asks Frederic, pointing at the apple. Journal shakes his head, and Frederic grabs the fruit, shoves it in his pocket, and hurries to the Left Bank of the river.

'Follow me,' orders the owner of the Alma Stables as soon as Frederic arrives.

As Frederic trails the owner to a long row of box stalls lining the back of a large courtyard, he catches sight of the top of the Eiffel Tower peeking over the rooftops.

Most Parisians don't like the wrought-iron tower, but Frederic's father had always loved it, right from the time it was constructed for the World's Fair twenty-one years ago – and for that reason alone, Frederic loves it too.

'Here he is,' says the stables' owner, reaching the last stall of the row. 'He's a big boy, strong and unpredictable. A former military horse, part Andalusian, part Percheron.'

'Former military?' Frederic asks excitedly. 'So he's used to being ridden?'

'If you're brave enough or stupid enough,' the owner says. 'He's got a temper. But because of his size and strength he'll be perfect for a four-horse team. Just right for the kind of carriage Gustave is thinking of buying.'

But Frederic isn't really listening. He's in awe of the striking grey stallion – its elegant head and long neck, its thick mane and tail, its massive chest and hindquarters. Frederic has never seen a more beautiful or athletic horse. With a pang of sorrow, he realises that he looks just like one of the horses from the painting in the Louvre.

'What's his name?' Frederic asks.

'That's horse number *onze*, eleven,' says the owner. Then noticing Frederic's perplexed look, he says, 'It's just a horse. It doesn't need a name.'

Frederic holds his tongue. Doesn't need a name? How absurd! he thinks, as he opens the stall and takes a step towards Eleven.

'Hey! Don't just walk in like that,' warns the owner. 'Let me get you a stick or a whip.'

Frederic is disgusted by the thought. He shakes his head.

Eleven snorts and rears backwards. The horse is skittish and wary, that's clear. And it easily weighs over a thousand pounds. Frederic knows that, if he wanted to, this stallion could charge and crush him. But he also knows that horses are sensitive creatures and can sense how you feel. And Frederic feels certain that the stallion knows he feels no fear and intends him no harm.

Frederic closes his eyes for a moment, takes in a deep breath, exhales, and then slowly takes a step towards Eleven.

He looks up at the stallion.

'I'm not going to hurt you,' he says in a soothing voice.

Eleven snorts a couple of times and then lowers his head.

Frederic reaches out and gently scratches him around the neck. 'Do you like that?' he says. He strokes Eleven's nose, then lightly rubs the bone above the stallion's eyes. Eleven's eyelids begin to droop, as if he's about to doze off.

'I don't believe it,' says the owner. 'I've never seen this horse so docile. You've almost put him to sleep.'

Frederic leads Eleven out onto the Paris streets. When he and the horse are a good distance away from the stables, and out of sight from the owner, Frederic turns to the stallion.

'Eleven is a dumb name for a grand horse like you,' he whispers. 'From now on, I'm calling you Charlemagne.'

une fouetté
ROUNDHOUSE KICK

Frederic comforts and chats to Charlemagne every step along the way. 'Ignore the traffic, boy,' Frederic whispers as they reach the busier streets.

Cutting ghostly figures in the grey drizzle, Frederic and Charlemagne make their way along the avenue.

Frederic notices a crowd gathering on the *Pont d'Alma* – Alma Bridge. Everyone is peering over the railing, looking at the river.

What's going on? Frederic wonders. He risks leading Charlemagne over to take a closer look.

From his jacket pocket Frederic pulls out Journal's apple and, as Charlemagne crunches on it, he approaches the crowd.

Frederic overhears people talking about the level of the river – the water is rising at a rapid rate. Frederic leans over to look. It's true – he has never seen the water so high. What's more, tree branches, boxes, barrels and other debris are bobbing in the fast current.

He looks up at the two stone statues of soldiers standing on pillars attached to the bridge. They are giant – as tall as eight big men standing on each other's shoulders. Usually the river flows just below the base on which the statues stand. One of the soldiers, the one closest to the right bank is a *Zouave* – a French colonial soldier holding a rifle. The river is lapping up around his waist!

Frederic wonders with alarm how much higher the river can rise.

He loops Charlemagne's lead rope to a nearby lamp post and presses up against the bridge railings to take a closer look.

From this height, when he turns to check on Charlemagne, he spots a boy, not much older than himself, circling the crowd. He looks suspicious – for one thing, he's the only one not paying any attention to the rising water.

The boy trips and bumps into a well-dressed man. But as the boy straightens and apologises, Frederic sees him reaching inside the man's coat. He snatches something that glints in the light before it vanishes into his sleeve.

It's the man's pocket watch, Frederic suddenly realises. The boy is a pickpocket!

'Thief,' Frederic mutters under his breath. Just the sight of this act triggers the memories of his father and the thieves at the Louvre. Frederic's heart pounds, and he feels anger bubbling throughout his entire body. But he also feels sick with guilt – and the guilt mixed in with anger makes him want to burst.

Without thinking, he shouts at the boy: 'Stop! You dirty rotten thief!'

The boy's eyes widen as he spots Frederic. The gentleman turns at the sound of Frederic's cry, pats his coat pocket and realises he has been robbed.

'My watch! My watch!' the man hollers after the boy, who bolts down the embankment.

But Frederic is right behind him, charging at him in full stride.

The boy stumbles and Frederic pounces. The two hit the cobblestones hard and roll down the street, wrestling furiously. They collide into a park bench and break apart.

Frederic hardly feels the pain. He springs to his feet.

They face each other with raised fists. The pickpocket is the first to lunge. He throws a right punch, but Frederic blocks him with an upper left-elbow deflection, followed by a powerful right-heel thrust to his gut.

The pickpocket doubles over, but only for a moment. He bounces up and pulls a dagger from his back pocket. Sneering, he swings the deadly blade at Frederic.

Frederic ducks, spins, and executes a *fouetté* – a roundhouse kick – directly at the boy, booting the weapon right out of his hand.

Before the pickpocket can make sense of what has happened, Frederic lets loose with six rapid, sharp punches at his face – left, right, left, right, left and right.

As the boy drops to the ground, dazed, Frederic jumps on his chest and pins him to the ground.

'Stay out of my business!' the boy growls, his teeth and nose bloodied. 'Wait until my gang hears about this. You're going to pay!'

As if snapping out of a trance, Frederic is surprised and shocked. How did this happen? He hasn't fought since that day in the boxing hall.

'Yeah, well, from where I sit, you're the one who's just paid,' Frederic tells him, retrieving the stolen watch from the boy's shirt pocket.

When he gets up, the boy spits at him and runs away.

Returning to the *Pont d'Alma*, Frederic scans the crowd and spots the gentleman.

'I don't believe it. That's remarkable. Thank you, young man. Thank you,' the man says, taking the watch from Frederic. 'Your heroic act needs to be rewarded!'

But as the man reaches inside his coat for his wallet, Frederic looks guiltily over to Charlemagne. The horse is safe but shifting nervously, still tethered to the lamp post.

'It's all right,' Frederic mutters. '*Ce n'était rien!* It was nothing! I must get back to work. Good day, Monsieur.'

Frederic hurriedly leads Charlemagne away.

l'inondation
FLOOD

The following morning Frederic wakes to his mother calling him. It's only just dawn. He bolts out of bed and is shocked to find himself splashing through a deep puddle of icy water.

'Arrgh!' Frederic yelps. '*Qu'est-ce que c'est*? What is this?'

'*L'inondation!* We're flooded!' his mother tells him as she rushes around packing their things. 'The whole apartment!' She splashes to the front door. 'It's not raining! Where's this water coming from?'

Frederic immediately thinks back to yesterday and the rising river. He wades outside and can't believe what he sees. The entire neighbourhood is flooded, and the streets have been transformed into canals. Neighbours are streaming out of their homes in a panic – shouting at one another. Some are calling for help.

'The entire city is flooded!' Someone yells from a few doors down. 'It's coming up from the ground.'

'How?' asks Frederic. 'How is that possible?'

'I heard the water is flooding the sewer tunnels and subway lines,' their neighbour cries. 'It's coming up from the basements, through sewer grates and manholes on the street.'

A man appears on a makeshift raft. Standing in his nightshirt in the bitterly cold water that has now reached his knees, Frederic is momentarily stunned.

'At least the river quay walls haven't broken,' says the man as he floats by. 'If they do break, it will be a disaster!'

'This is incredible,' says Frederic. 'It's like a dream.'

'Hey, boy!'

Frederic looks up to the balcony grannies.

'You're going to catch yourself a deadly cold,' says one of the grannies.

'Or typhoid fever!' says the other.

'Are you both okay?' asks Frederic. 'Do you need help?'

'We don't need help, boy! Thank heavens we're on

the second floor. We're toasty dry and we're not going anywhere. And they're not going to make us.'

Frederic follows the balcony grannies' gaze to see horse-drawn police wagons, firefighters and the French Society for Assistance to Wounded Soldiers, the SBBM for short, at the far end of his street.

Some police are checking on residents and the others are positioning wooden gangplanks to create *passerelles* – makeshift footbridges and walkways – so people don't have to wade through the rising water.

Frederic steps back inside to find his mother desperately stuffing clothes into suitcases and moving valuables to the top of the cupboards, out of reach of the water.

'Hurry up and get dressed,' she says. 'I have no idea what we're going to do. Where are we going to sleep? Are we now homeless, like the vagabonds on the street? If I don't look clean and presentable, I will lose my job.'

'The SBBM are in our street,' Frederic says, as he sits on his bed, dries his feet and changes into his clothes. 'I can go and ask them . . .'

'No!' says his mother. 'You stay right where you are, young man, where I know you're safe. Oh, dear God, what are we going to do?'

Frederic can see the stress and helplessness on

his mother's face. He understands why. There are no relatives nearby to help, and even though they can't stay in their apartment, they will still need to pay the rent.

'It's okay, *Maman*. We'll work something out,' says Frederic, doing his best to comfort her. Just then there's a rap at the door.

Frederic opens the door to a SBBM officer.

'Churches and schools in the elevated parts of the city have been turned into shelters,' he says. 'We're here to take you to Saint Nicholas's church hall in the third *arrondissement*, the third district. It's a shelter just for women and children. So your husband would have to go to a shelter for men at the –'

'There's no husband to be concerned about,' Frederic's mother says bluntly. 'And we're ready to go now.'

Several minutes later Frederic and his mother and two stuffed suitcases are being bundled onto the back of a large horse-drawn wagon. They squeeze in between other mothers and their children, all tightly packed in. Frederic recognises a few of the faces from other streets in his neighbourhood, but not well enough to talk to them.

'Wait!' he cries, as they are about to set off for the shelter. 'I forgot something!'

Frederic jumps off the wagon, wades back inside, and springs onto his bed. Hanging on a hook on the wall above his bed is the Eagle, the kite his parents bought him for his birthday. He unties it and runs back to the wagon. No one knows how much higher the river is expected to rise. And Frederic doesn't want to risk losing his most treasured possession – the only thing he has left of his father.

As the wagon slowly sloshes through the flooded streets, there's an eerie silence as they watch the drama unfold in front of them. Frederic has never seen anything like it.

There are people chasing after their belongings as they float away in the murky water. Restaurant and store-owners sob outside their businesses as they watch the rising water soak and ruin their stock and food supplies.

In the lower streets, in the distance, they can see people hanging from second and third floor windows yelling for help – while others try to reach them with tall ladders.

Ahead of them, a woman is clinging to a man's back to stay dry and another man is wading through the water on stilts. Frederic almost smiles.

But the flood is no joke. Thousands of people will be out of work, businesses will be ruined and thousands and thousands of people will be homeless.

In a badly flooded street, Frederic spots Leon, splashing through the water.

He calls out to him. 'I'm going to a shelter, but then I'll make my way to the stables!'

'Don't bother!' Leon calls back. 'The stables are flooded, and Gustave is trying to find another stable to house the horses. Find us once the flood subsides – if it subsides!'

Frederic sighs. 'Now what?' he asks his mother.

But she doesn't know what lies ahead and nor does anyone else.

un grand héros
A BIG HERO

When the wagon reaches Saint Nicholas's Church, a nun in a grey tunic, with a white cowl and veil over her face, tells Frederic and his mother to join a long line of other flood victims. They slowly make their way into a large hall next door.

It's packed. Rows of thin mattresses cover the floor and people take up every square metre. SBBM workers are handing out blankets and pillows and packages of bread and cheese.

A man directs Frederic and his mother to their small corner of the hall. Even though there are so many people crammed together in the hall, it's strangely quiet.

Frederic's mother gets right to work making their beds and unpacking. She uses the empty suitcases to create a divide between them and other evacuees.

'What's the rush?' asks Frederic miserably, standing his kite up beside his makeshift bed. 'It's not like we're going anywhere.'

'Speak for yourself,' Frederic's mother snaps. 'I still need to work. I hope Madame will understand why I'm late. Are you going to be all right? I heard they'll be giving out more food packages throughout the day.'

Frederic nods, but he's distracted by a girl who looks dishevelled and helpless at the other end of the hall. It looks as if she's being bullied by a boy – they are fighting over a blanket.

'Frederic?' his mother snaps. 'Did you hear me? Are you going to be all right?'

'Yes, *Maman*. I'll be all right,' says Frederic, now wondering if he will be.

Frederic's mother kisses him on the forehead and leaves. Frederic immediately makes his way through the crowded hall over to the girl.

'I've got this one!' says the boy, tugging forcefully at the blanket.

'It's mine!' cries the girl.

'Give her the blanket!' Frederic says, stepping up

to the boy. 'Or else you'll have me to deal with.'

Alarmed, the boy releases his grip on the blanket and the girl goes flying. She falls backwards onto her bottom.

Frederic tries to help her back to her feet, but she slaps his hand away.

'What do you think you're doing?' she snaps, brushing down her wrinkled coat and dress.

'I was only trying to help,' says Frederic. 'You're welcome by the way.'

'You're welcome?' scoffs the girl. 'Oh, thank you, Great Prince, for coming to my rescue. Ha!'

Frederic is taken aback. 'Are you mocking me?' he asks. 'You looked as if you were in trouble. And when someone's in trouble, you either stand back or you show some courage and –'

'Be a knight in shining armour? *Un grand héros*, a big hero?' The girl grins and shakes her head. She has deep dimples and big green eyes. 'Well, thank you, big hero. But I wasn't in trouble.'

The girl looks to the other boy. 'What's your name again?'

The boy's plump cheeks flush bright red. 'Thierry,' he says.

'I challenged Thierry to a tug-of-war. To see who was stronger. I am, of course.'

'Oh, ' says Frederic, feeling a little foolish. 'Then I'll leave you alone.'

'Hey!' the girl says. 'I bet I'm stronger than you too. I challenge you to a game. Come on!'

'*Non merci, pas pour moi* – no, thanks, not for me,' says Frederic, turning back to his corner of the shelter.

'Is the big hero frightened of a girl beating him?' says the girl.

Frederic doesn't answer. He's baffled by her. How can she be so lighthearted when everyone else is miserable? he thinks. Isn't she worried about her flooded home?

'Ooh, so serious!' she adds. 'I'm Claire. And you are?'

'Frederic.'

'This is Thierry,' she says, turning to the boy. 'I just met him. Isn't that right, Thierry?'

'Yes, yes. I'm Thierry Bonneville. Can I just say that was incredibly gallant of you to come to try and rescue Claire, *comme ça*, like that. Like a dashing character from a novel.'

Thierry scribbles something into a small note-book.

'What are you doing?' asks Frederic.

'I'm writing. I like to record things. It might make

63

for a good story one day,' he says. 'I'm going to be a famous novelist like Alexandre Dumas. I've read his novel *The Three Musketeers* twice and I'm going to read *The Count of Monte Cristo* next. I hope all my books are not ruined. I put them on the very top of the kitchen cupboard, so I hope the water won't reach them.'

'Are you here with your mother?' asks Claire.

Frederic nods and explains that his mother had to go to work.

'Did your father have to go to another shelter?' asks Claire.

Frederic shakes his head. 'My father, um . . .' He stutters, unable to finish the sentence.

'No longer around?' says Claire.

'Yeah.' Frederic nods.

'Me too!' Thierry says. 'He was a builder. He died in a construction accident when I was young, so I didn't really know him. *Maman* also had to go to work today. She works as a chambermaid at the Hotel Christophe-Antoine. That's a new fancy hotel in *Saint-Germain-des-Prés*.'

'What about your mother?' Frederic asks Claire.

'She's somewhere over there.' Claire points to a group of women standing by the entrance to the shelter. 'She's helping the nuns hand out blankets.'

Frederic looks, but there are about five women and none of them look much like Claire.

He's distracted by an elderly lady who is crying as she's being helped into the shelter. He watches a nun trying to comfort her. But the woman sobs even more.

'What's happened?' Frederic asks another nun, standing close by.

'Her cat, Renoir, is still back at her flooded home,' explains the nun. 'It seems Renoir ran away when the SBBM came to pick up Madame – and she's terribly concerned for him.'

Claire smiles. 'Frederic can go get her cat for her!' she says.

'Really?' the nun says. 'You would do that?'

'Of course he would do that.' Claire proclaims. 'He's a hero, ready to serve, and he'll be more than happy to rescue the cat. Isn't that right, Frederic?'

'Really?' Frederic says, glaring at Claire. 'I don't hear you offering to go back into the floodwaters.'

He turns back to the nun. 'I can do that,' he says. 'But every hero needs sidekicks, so these two are coming with me.'

le secours
THE RESCUE

'Isn't this exciting?' says Thierry, running behind Claire and Frederic as they move in single file along the *passerelles* with the water lapping below.

Frederic has to agree with Thierry – there's something exciting about getting around the city this way. Although many of the pedestrians, mostly the elderly people, are finding it difficult as they shuffle carefully along the narrow gangplanks. Some people are holding onto each other for balance, slowing up those behind them. Up ahead they hear shrieks as four people slip and tumble into the cold water.

He's surprised to see that many people seem to be carrying on as if it's a normal day – going to work and running their errands, making deposits at the banks that are still open and posting letters in the unflooded parts of the city.

'Here it is! The old lady's street,' announces Claire. '*Rue Moreau*.'

There are no *passerelles* in this street, and Frederic takes a deep breath before stepping down into the waist-deep water.

'Ah!' Thierry grimaces. 'It's freeeezing!'

'Oh, come on!' says Claire, wading ahead. 'It won't kill you.'

'Um, it might!' says Thierry. 'I think I read somewhere that very cold water can have a negative effect on the body. Maybe it was in Jules Verne's *Twenty Thousand Leagues Under the Sea*. Now *that's* an adventure. If you haven't read it you should because –'

'Here's the address!' says Frederic, unlocking the front door and pushing it open. It was difficult against the floodwaters. 'Let's hope Renoir is back.'

Frederic, Claire and Thierry wade through the apartment. In the front room every wall is covered by butterflies – a huge collection in boxed frames. More are hanging on the hallway walls and sitting on the mantle.

'Look at all of them!' says Frederic.

'Beautiful,' says Thierry.

'Kind of creepy, if you ask me,' says Claire. 'Renoir!'

'Renoir! Renoir! Here, Renoir!' they call out in unison.

But there's no cat in sight.

'Well, so much for being a heroic trio,' sighs Thierry. 'I was even thinking of what we could call ourselves. Something like the Amazing Rain Gang.'

Frederic laughs and Claire rolls her eyes.

'No?' says Thierry. 'I'll keep thinking then. He reaches for a large butterfly net on the top of a bookcase.

'I love this,' says Thierry, swishing it in the air. 'I wish I had one.'

'Well, I don't think her cat is here,' says Frederic, wading out from the bedroom. 'She'll be so disappointed that we couldn't find him.'

'Wait a minute,' says Claire. 'I think I can hear him.'

Loud meowing is coming from the street.

Through the window, Frederic notices something floating in the middle of the road.

'I think it's Renoir!' he cries.

Balanced unhappily on a piece of floating debris is a black-and-white cat, meowing at the top of its lungs. Renoir is bedraggled and soaking wet, his bottom half dangling in the murky water.

The three rush outside and wade in the direction of the cat. But they are stopped by shouting coming from the other end of the street.

Frederic, Claire and Thierry turn to see men in three rowboats paddling frantically towards them.

'*Attention! Attention!* Crocodile! Crocodile!'

'What are they shouting?' asks Claire.

'It sounds as if they're saying crocodile,' says Frederic. 'But they can't be, can they? Why would there be a crocodile?'

'They *are* saying crocodile!' Thierry hollers. 'LOOK!'

Frederic turns just in time to see what looks like a log breaking the surface of the water down the street. It's moving in their direction. But it's not a log. It has small beady eyes and a snout. A crocodile! In the middle of Paris!

'It's heading for Renoir!' cries Thierry.

'He's dinner and we'll be dessert if we don't get out of here,' Claire says, wading back in the direction of the shouting men. 'Come on! What are you waiting for? Let's go!'

Thierry turns and splashes towards Claire, but Frederic wades back into the old lady's house. The floodwater swirls about his waist, sucking the litter, debris and even floating pillows in his wake.

Frederic snatches the butterfly net where Thierry

left it and heads back outside.

He charges in the direction of Renoir – and the reptilian predator. He has no time to think whether he is scared or not. All he knows is he has to show the type of courage and bravery his father expected of him. There's no way he's letting any one else down. Not even Renoir.

'Are you crazy?' Claire shouts out to him.

'Maybe!' he yells back.

Frederic splashes through the icy water, holding the end of the butterfly net out in front of him like a knight charging with a lance.

The crocodile is only seconds away from making Renoir its lunch.

With only a metre separating them, Frederic throws himself forward and smacks the pole across the surface of the water in front of the crocodile's snout.

It spooks the reptile, who flicks its tail and shoots off in the opposite direction.

But only for a moment. In seconds, the crocodile has turned and is heading back towards them.

Frederic scoops Renoir up in the butterfly net.

But Renoir is not thrilled to be rescued. He thrashes about, hissing and yowling. The pole bends, and Frederic hopes it won't break.

Frederic may understand horses, but he knows nothing about cats, especially terrified ones that look like they want to scratch your eyeballs out. It's difficult to wade quickly in waist-deep water with Renoir twisting and flipping himself into knots in the net. But somehow Frederic manages to charge back in the direction of Claire and Thierry, who have now joined the men in the boats.

When he reaches them his heart feels as if it's going to burst out of his chest.

'Here, take him!' says Frederic, swinging the net over the boat.

'No way!' Thierry says. 'That thing looks more vicious than the crocodile!'

Frederic panics. 'Well, I don't have all day!'

One of the men hurriedly grabs a blanket and scoops Renoir up – and Frederic flings himself into the rowboat.

'That was incredible!' gasps Claire.

'And seriously stupid,' says one of the other men in the boat.

Frederic notices the men are all wearing uniforms with the emblems of the Paris Zoo.

'These men say that crocodiles have escaped from the zoo and are swimming in the Seine,' Thierry says, writing frantically in his notebook. 'You couldn't make things like this up!'

'Only two crocodiles,' corrects one of the zoo offi-cials. 'We already got one back, but we still need to capture Beatrice.'

'Beatrice? Really? Beatrice the crocodile – bril-liant!' Thierry scribbles frantically.

Frederic watches as the other two boats filled with zoo workers and firefighters corral the crocodile. It's not long before they've captured Beatrice with the help of large fishing nets and hooped ropes.

'Well, our first rescue will be hard to top, *n'est-ce pas*? Right?' Claire says to Frederic and Thierry. She's holding a much calmer Renoir in her arms and drying him with the blanket. 'So what's next, big hero?'

'What do you mean, what's next?' asks Frederic, as they're dropped off in a non-flooded street.

'Who or what are we going to rescue next?' Claire says. 'We're not going to stop now, are we?'

'No, no, we can't stop!' Thierry blurts. 'This is just the beginning for the Crocodile Crusaders.'

He looks up hopefully to see what the others think of the name.

Claire shakes her head.

Frederic sighs.

He shrugs. 'Anyway if we're really going to help

those in trouble in this flood we're going to need a boat.'

'Simple!' Claire grins as they approach the entrance of the Saint Nicholas shelter. 'I know where we can get one.'

le bateau
THE BOAT

Frederic struggles to sleep in the shelter. It's cold, bitterly cold. And trying to sleep with several hundred people crammed in the same space isn't easy.

Most people are wrapped in blankets. Many are huddled together by the heating stations that have been set up throughout the hall – makeshift ovens with cut-out holes and burning kindling inside.

It's dawn, and Frederic hops up from his bed, sneaks past his mother, and makes his way to warm his hands by one of the heating stations. He spots Thierry on the other side of the hall. Thierry smiles and carefully walks around the sleeping people on the floor to join him.

'*Bonjour, mon ami!* Good morning, my friend!' Thierry whispers. 'I slept so well. Did you?'

Frederic shakes his head. 'No,' he says, 'How could you, with all the snoring, coughing and farting?'

'I could even sleep through a thunderstorm,' Thierry says, rubbing his hands and breathing into his palms. 'I like waking up early too. I'd be getting ready for school now, but my school is closed, at least until the flood is over. What about you, do you go to school?'

Frederic tells Thierry how he now works, or at least used to work. Thierry is a year younger and in his final year at primary school.

'Hey! Enough gas-bagging. Let's go!'

It's Claire, popping up out of nowhere.

'Where did you come from?' Frederic asks, looking back over his shoulder. 'Where did you sleep? I tried to find you last night but couldn't see you anywhere.'

'Well, I was here,' says Claire. 'At the other end of the hall.'

'With your mother? Is she going to work today?' Thierry asks.

'What is this? An interrogation?' Claire snaps. '*Maman* sells flowers at Les Halles market. She's already gone for the day. I thought we agreed that first thing this morning I would take you to get a boat.

What are we waiting for? Let's go see who needs our help! Oh, and here, one each . . .'

Claire takes two small baguettes out of a paper bag and hands one each to Frederic and Thierry.

'Where'd you get these?' asks Thierry. 'They're still warm!'

'More questions?' says Claire. 'Well, if you must know I got them from a bakery giving out free bread to flood victims. It's their way of doing something for those in need.' She grins. 'Why am I even explaining this to you? Come on.'

—

'Are we there yet?' Thierry complains.

'If you ask me that one more time, I'm going to dunk you into the river,' Claire tells him.

Frederic has convinced them that they should visit the *Pont d'Alma* to take a look at the water level of the river.

He gasps when he sees the river. The water rushing under the bridge is now flowing up to the chest of the *Zouave* soldier statue.

They cross the bridge onto the Left Bank and backtrack along the river towards the *Gare d'Orsay*.

Frederic is in awe of the lavish train station and

its immense columns, grand arches, and vast barrel-shaped dome ceiling.

But he's aghast to see that it is mostly underwater.

A large crowd of onlookers stream in to take a look.

Frederic, Thierry and Claire wait their turn like tourists and eventually reach the front of the crowd. It looks less like a station and more like a giant swimming pool. All the tracks are completely submerged.

'Come on, this way,' instructs Claire, leading Frederic and Thierry back outside.

Claire takes the boys a couple of blocks past the station, down a narrow laneway and through a hole in a wooden gate in a stone wall. When they pop out the other side, they find themselves in the middle of a junkyard filled with old train carriages, horse-wagons, scrap metal and clumps of wood – most of it underwater.

Claire heads directly for one of the train carriages. She steps inside and the boys cautiously follow. Lying on the aisle of the carriage is a small rowboat, with one oar inside. There are a couple of blankets folded up inside the boat – as if someone has been sleeping there.

'How did you even know this was here?' asks Thierry. 'You've obviously been here before. Why?

Why would you want to come to a junkyard like this?'

'Why do you ask so many questions?' Claire snaps.

Thierry shrugs, but his questions make Frederic look at Claire in a new light. For the first time he notices how mismatched her clothes are – her coat is a size too big and her boots look as if they were made for a boy. Her dress is frayed at the hem. Her brown hair is done up in a bun, but loosely, as if she did it in a rush or doesn't have enough pins to hold it all together – she has wispy bits hanging across her face.

'Are we going to use this boat or what?' she adds.

The boys nod.

Claire directs them to help her drag the boat out of the junkyard and down towards the flooded streets. Once they get to water deep enough, they hop aboard, wobbling a little as they find their balance.

Frederic gets the hang of it in no time and starts paddling with the single oar.

'Yes!' cries Thierry excitedly. 'We're rowing – in the city! We're the Rowing Renegades of Paris! What do you think? Catchy, no?'

Frederic laughs and shakes his head.

'No!' Claire says.

The three paddle around the streets, looking for people who might need their help. No one needs rescuing, but they end up providing taxi rides. They transport a lady with a bag filled with kindling to her home on the second floor of an apartment. They offer a ride to a man and his dog. They cart a musician and his cello to his music studio on a hill. And a Swiss tourist offers them one whole franc just for a joyride.

'So much for being heroes,' sighs Claire. 'We're nothing but a transport and sightseeing service. Boooor-ing.'

'Yes, this can't compare with saving defenceless cats from the snapping jaws of marauding crocodiles,' Thierry adds.

'Said like a true writer!' Frederic grins, continuing to paddle.

'Oh no!' cries Thierry. 'Look! We have to rescue them!'

Up ahead hundreds of books are floating and bobbing up and down the street.

Thierry leans over the side of the boat and begins scooping up as many as he can grab. Claire assists him, tossing one waterlogged volume after another into the bottom of the boat.

'Oh my lord!' Thierry panics. 'The greatest French writers of our time are drowning!'

Frederic thinks Thierry's reaction is a bit over the top. He's never met anyone so in love with books before. 'Not too many!' he says. 'We'll sink!'

'It's Victor Hugo's *Les Misérables*!' says Thierry in a choked voice, trying to fan out the wet pages of the novel. 'And there's Flaubert's *Madame Bovary*! And Stendahl's *Le Rouge et le Noir*! And . . .'

The shops lining the streets here are still busy with people – bakeries and cafés are operating and boards have been added, joining the shops to the *passerelles* in the street, so people can come in without getting their feet wet.

Over Thierry's shoulder, Frederic spots a man stepping out from a café.

He's familiar, but Frederic can't place him. As he rows closer the man looks up, and it suddenly hits him.

It's the thief from the Louvre!

les souvenirs
MEMORIES

Frederic drops the oar and lunges out of the boat. He hardly hears Claire and Thierry calling after him or feels the biting cold of the water as he splashes across the flooded street, his heart racing and his teeth clenched.

The man turns a corner into another street, but by the time Frederic reaches the corner the man is nowhere to be seen.

Where did he go?

Frederic wades to the middle of the road, feeling frantic. He looks back and forth, scanning the windows of cafés and restaurants.

Pedestrians shuffling single file along the *passerelles*

are staring at him, bemused.

'Get out of the water, you fool!' a man says.

Frederic is overwhelmed. 'NO! NO! NO!' he mutters. He sighs heavily, feeling lost and angry and unsure of what to do next.

'Hey!' Claire cries, as she and Thierry finally catch up to him. 'What's going on?'

Frederic wipes the tears from his eyes and turns back to face them. He wonders if he has imagined it all.

But it *was* him, he tells himself. He had the same streak of white running through his hair.

'Are you okay?' Claire asks, as she glides the boat up along Frederic, who is now shivering, waist-deep in the water.

'Yeah,' he lies, as they pull him back into the rowboat.

'Who were you chasing after?' asks Thierry. 'You look really upset. What's happening? Can you tell us?'

'I'm sorry, I shouldn't have bolted like that,' Frederic says. 'I might explain later, but I can't right now.'

Frederic feels Claire watching him closely as Thierry paddles back towards the books.

'Hello!' cries a woman standing in the water in

front of the bookstore. She is waving to them. 'We saw you saving some of our books.'

The owners of the bookstore introduce themselves to Frederic and his friends as Monsieur and Madame Martin. They have been away and have only just returned. When they opened the door to their flooded store, the books floated out into the street.

'I'm afraid it's too late to save them,' says Madame Martin. 'But thank you for trying. Come upstairs and have some lunch.'

In the apartment above the shop, Madame Martin makes some hot onion soup and Frederic dries himself by the gas oven.

Thierry is so excited that he can't stop talking.

'Have you read every single book in your store? Is that even possible? I know I would!' he says excitedly. 'I spend so much time at the Sainte Genevieve library. That's where I read most of my books. One day I hope my novel will end up on the shelves of every library and bookstore. I'm going to write a story about the flood and my adventures with my two friends here.'

'Oh, how wonderful,' says Madame Martin, placing some bread on the table. 'Henri, did you hear that? We have a writer at our table.'

'Yes, yes, I heard,' says Monsieur Martin. 'And a modest one too!' he says, winking at Frederic and Claire.

There is a knock at the door and as Madame Martin answers it, Frederic sees a police officer standing there.

His heart almost stops. His mind instantly goes back to his father lying on the floor, motionless. He relives the experience of running across the museum to find another guard. And the time spent back by his father's side waiting for the police.

He hoped they would help him, but they had taken him away and he'd never seen his father again. They kept him at the station and asked him to repeat what happened again and again – relentless questioning but ultimately nothing came of it. No leads, nothing.

The officer at the door, dressed smartly in a navy blue woollen tunic with silver buttons and a cape and cap, is asking questions about the rowboat tied up below and the Martins let him in so Frederic and his friends can answer.

'No one owns it,' Thierry blurts, causing Claire to glare at him. 'We found it in a junkyard. Actually Claire found it.'

Claire shoots another look at Thierry and shakes her head at Frederic as if to say, '*Oh la vache!* Holy cow! He has a big mouth!'

'So you did steal the boat?' asks the officer, taking out a writing pad from his pocket.

'No!' Frederic says. 'We . . . um, no. We didn't steal it. We didn't think anyone owned it so I guess we were just borrowing it, so we could help people in trouble.'

'It's true, officer,' Madame Martin says. 'Don't be hard on them. These kids tried to do a good deed for us.'

'Oooh, I like that,' says Thierry, pulling out his notebook and pencil and scribbling. Over his shoulder Frederic sees him write *The Good Deed Trio*.

'I won't report you,' the officer says. 'But the boat is now the property of the Paris police. The city is under so much strain and I've spent the last couple of days chasing after looters. We need every boat we can muster. If it really isn't stolen, I will contact you again after the floods have gone down. Or you can come to see me at my depot in *Place de l'Opera*. I'm Officer Pierre. What are your full names?'

'Thierry Bonneville!' Thierry says enthusiastically.

'I'm Claire,' says Claire. 'Claire Fignon.'

'And I'm Frederic Lefosse,' adds Frederic.

'Lefosse?' the officer looks up from his notebook, interested. 'Why do I know that name?'

He chews the end of his pencil thoughtfully.

'That's it!' he cries. 'Lefosse! A guard at the Louvre was killed trying to thwart a robbery last summer.

The thieves got away with a Raphael painting. Was that Monsieur Lefosse any relation to you?'

Frederic freezes. Everyone is staring.

He looks at Claire. She looks at him as if she already knows the answer.

'Yes,' Frederic says softly. 'Claude Lefosse was my father.'

les amis
FRIENDS

Everyone is sympathetic and kind. But Frederic doesn't want to talk about his father. Or that night in the Louvre. He contemplates telling Officer Pierre about having just spotted the thief earlier – but he has begun to doubt himself and he's in no mood to be dragged to a station for more questioning.

He rushes Claire and Thierry to leave. Soon they say goodbye to the Martins and are back outside in the bleak wintry weather, walking in single file along the *passerelles*.

There's silence for most of the way as they patiently stop and start and pass pedestrians on the gangplanks – although Frederic can tell that both

Thierry and Claire are desperate to say something. He can feel their stares burning into the back of his head.

'What?' he suddenly stops and turns to face them. Thierry bumps into Frederic and almost falls off the planks. Claire grabs him and he regains his balance just in time.

'Go on, say what you have to say!' says Frederic.

'We're sorry, that's all,' Thierry says softly.

'Yeah, we are,' says Claire. 'That man you chased after, did he have something to do with your father's death?'

Frederic is taken aback by Claire's directness. Not only does she have gumption, she's also very sharp.

'Yes.' Frederic feels overcome with emotion. 'I can't stop thinking about it. It *was* him. I will never forget what he looks like. He was the man who killed my father.'

'What? No way.' Thierry goes to grab his notebook from his jacket pocket, but is stopped by Claire slapping her hand on his chest.

'Are you sure?' asks Claire.

'No, I can't be sure he's the man who killed my father, but he was there,' says Frederic. 'I wasn't in the room – I should've been! I should've been there to save him, but I wasn't.'

'Why didn't you say something to the officer?' Claire asks.

'I don't really know why,' says Frederic bitterly. 'But even if I had, it wouldn't have made any difference. You think the police can help you, Claire, but they can't. They don't.'

Suddenly Frederic hears a scream. It sounds as though it's coming from the next street.

Without hesitation Frederic, Claire and Thierry swing into action. They jump off the *passerelles*, splash through the watery *rue de Grenelle* and dart into one of the high dry streets, the *rue du Bac*.

A woman is holding onto a baby and is standing crying over an open manhole. There are other people gathering, but no one seems to be doing anything.

'My boy has fallen,' she sobs. 'He's only little! Oh, dear God, help me! It might be too late.'

Frederic pushes past some of the gawkers in front of him and runs to the open manhole. He looks into the darkness below and scrambles down the iron ladder attached to the side of the narrow shaft. Halfway down he begins to hear faint cries for help.

At the bottom of the shaft is a large brick sewer tunnel, and running through it is a raging stream of water. Frederic climbs down the ladder until half of his body is submerged beneath the wild rapids.

He tightens his grip on the ladder, and looks across the tunnel – but it's dark and difficult to see. After a moment Frederic's eyes adjust and he sees the boy.

On the same side of the tunnel, about three metres down from Frederic, the boy is in the water gripping precariously to another iron ladder attached to the tunnel wall.

The boy's face is only just above the water. He sees Frederic and his eyes widen. He bursts into tears – and Frederic can see that he won't be able to hold on much longer.

Frederic takes off his jacket, and holds onto one of the arms of the coat. It's difficult while holding on to a ladder. He tosses the other end of the coat towards the boy.

'Grab it!' Frederic calls out to him, but the coat smacks against the surface of the gushing murky water.

The boy tries to reach the arm of the coat, but the torrent is just too strong and the jacket too short.

Frederic's heart is racing.

'I've got an idea!' comes a voice from above.

Frederic is startled to see that Claire is now in the manhole shaft, standing a couple of ladder rungs above him.

'Here!' she yells, handing another coat to him. 'It's Thierry's.'

Frederic takes the coat from Claire, hooks his arm around the ladder rung and ties the two coat arms together.

'This could work,' he yells. He once again throws the coat-rope.

The boy swipes for it. But again, the coat falls short and he misses.

Frederic tries again, and again. But he just can't reach him. And the boy is rapidly losing the strength to hold on. His face drops beneath the gushing water for a moment.

'No! No!' Frederic yells at him. 'Look at me! We'll get you out! Don't let go. You must hold on!'

'Frederic!' Claire calls.

Frederic looks up to see that Thierry has also climbed down the shaft and is just above Claire.

'Take my braces!' Thierry cries, unclipping them from his trousers and passing them onto Claire, who passes them onto Frederic.

'Yes! Brilliant!' Frederic says, tying the braces onto one of the arms of the coat.

Frederic gets into position again to cast the coat-rope. 'Here goes!'

The boy throws out his arm and this time manages

to grasp one of the braces' straps.

'Yes!' Frederic cries, hoping that his knots will hold. 'Hold on!'

Frederic begins to drag the boy back, but he's straining to pull him through the strong current and with one arm wrapped around the ladder he doesn't have much strength.

'Here! Let me help!' Claire calls, leaning towards Frederic. 'Remember I'm a champion when it comes to tug-of-war.'

Frederic gives her part of the coat arm and together they tug as hard as they can.

'It's working!' Frederic calls, as the boy is pulled closer to him.

'Just a little bit more. Almost, almost . . . Yes!'

Frederic leans forward and grabs the boy. He grabs at them too – and with Claire and Thierry's help they manage to get him back up the ladder to safety.

—

A large crowd has now surrounded the entrance of the manhole and everyone cheers loudly as the woman embraces her son and the fire brigade arrive in their horse-drawn truck.

'That was amazing, *mes amis!*' Claire says to Frederic as the firemen wrap them in blankets.

'*You're* fantastic!' Frederic tells her. 'Good thinking grabbing the other coat.'

Frederic and Claire exchange smiles while Thierry takes out his notebook and scribbles: 'And the young heroes come to the rescue again, but heaven only knows what lies ahead for Fearless Frederic and his Floodwater Friends.'

l'énigme
THE PUZZLE

Frederic, Thierry and Claire draw some attention back at the shelter when the firemen drop them off and they recount the story to the nuns and the evacuees.

Thierry is doing most of the talking, as everyone shuffles in closer to listen. Thierry is the perfect storyteller, Frederic thinks. He knows when to pause and when to raise his voice during the exciting bits. And he loves the attention his story brings.

Once the story is over and everyone else disperses, the three friends huddle together around the heating stations while the nuns dart back and forth to find food and extra blankets.

'You're thinking of your father, right?' Claire asks Frederic.

Frederic nods.

'He would've been proud of you today,' Claire adds.

Frederic shrugs but he appreciates Claire's kind words. No one has ever said this to him before, and he wonders if his father *would* be proud of him.

Yes, he would, he thinks. He would've liked that we showed courage and didn't hold back. But Frederic thinks of that night in the museum again and is hit with a wave of regret.

'My father would have been proud of me,' says Thierry, warming his hands by the fire. 'I think he would've been proud of us all. I really miss him.'

Frederic knows how that feels. Not a day passes by without him thinking of his father.

'*Et toi*, Claire? And you?' Thierry asks.

Frederic half expects Claire to snap at Thierry and change the subject, but she doesn't.

'I don't have a father,' she says honestly and directly.

There's silence. The three sit with their own thoughts and listen to the fire crackling in the heating drum.

A few minutes later, Frederic's mother runs through the door and hugs him tightly.

'Whatever made you do it?' she asks. 'I was just

told! A boy was trapped down a flooded sewer tunnel and you climbed down there? Are you hurt?'

'No,' says Frederic, squished in his mother's embrace. 'I'm all right, *Maman*.'

'Thank heavens you are!' she says, annoyed and relieved at the same time. 'You're all I have! Don't you ever put your life in danger like that again. And don't think I don't know what you're doing. Your father would've wanted you to be safe. Got that? Now let's go and settle in for the night.'

'See you in the morning,' Thierry says. 'My mother will be back soon too.' He walks to his side of the hall.

Frederic gets up to follow his mother back to their bedding, but when he looks back over his shoulder to wave at Claire he sees the look on her face. She looks forlorn and almost teary.

'Are you all right?' he asks.

'Yes,' she answers, still seated. 'Don't worry about me. My mother will be here soon. Have a good night, big hero. See you in the morning.'

—

In the morning, Frederic sets out early to check on their home. There's been talk throughout the shelter that looting is on the increase across the city. Shops and abandoned homes are being robbed. He also has the job of seeing that the balcony grannies are safe and have enough food.

'Hopefully that will keep you out of trouble,' his mother tells him as she leaves for work.

Thierry offers to come along.

'Do you think we can avoid getting wet today, Frederic?' Thierry says, following closely behind him on the *passerelles*. 'The water seems to be subsiding a little so I'm hoping to stay dry. Claire must've gotten up really early because I was awake before dawn and I didn't see her. Did you? Do you think she went with her mother to sell flowers?'

'Thierry, please! Take a breath!' Frederic says. 'I don't know and I can't answer everything at once anyway. I guess Claire had things to do.'

Thierry is quiet for a second. 'Have you actually *seen* her mother?' he asks.

Frederic thinks about it. He hasn't. He wonders how much of what Claire says is in fact true. He shakes his head. 'No, but I'm sure we'll meet her later at some point.'

'I guess so,' Thierry says. 'Claire is definitely an *énigme*.'

'A what?' asks Frederic.

'A mystery, a puzzle – hard to work out,' Thierry explains.

'Yeah, I suppose she is,' Frederic says, spotting a young taxi driver outside a hotel. He is obviously having a hard time settling a skittish horse. It's a big grey beautiful stallion . . .

'Charlemagne!' Frederic exclaims.

'Charlemagne?' Thierry repeats. 'What?'

Frederic jumps off the *passerelles* and splashes across in the direction of the horse.

'So much for not getting wet!' Thierry calls out, chasing after him.

Frederic slowly approaches Charlemagne. The horse's head is raised high and he is stepping from side to side, clearly agitated. The groom is pulling on the reins trying to settle him and to make him stand in the one spot.

'What a magnificent beast,' Thierry says. 'It has the same colouring as Marengo – Napoleon's horse – although Marengo was a lot smaller!'

Frederic has almost forgotten how tall the stallion stands – he towers over them.

'It's okay, boy,' Frederic says, taking the horse's bridle and gently stroking the side of his face.

'*Merci, merci!*' says the groom, hopping off the wagon and onto the street. 'Frederic! Hello!'

'Leon?' Frederic says, happy to see him. 'I didn't recognise you with your driver's cap over your face.'

'It's so good to see you,' he cries. 'You know our *Grêler*, Hail, he just won't settle. He shouldn't be on a single cab, but we're so short on horses. Because of the flood we're busier than we've ever been. Horses handle watery streets better than cars. Some motor cars can't even work in the rain.'

'Hail?'

'That's what my uncle's named the horse.'

Frederic introduces Thierry to Leon – and makes a mental note to ask Thierry more about Marengo at another time.

'How's your home?' asks Leon. 'We were able to move the horses to the Fayette Stables up in the tenth *arrondissement*. The water is starting to go down at our stables, so hopefully it won't be too long before we'll be able to return – and then you can come back to work.'

'Thank you. I'm glad to hear that,' says Frederic. 'My home is still underwater. That's where I'm heading now, to check on it.'

Frederic pats Charlemagne before he and Thierry leave Leon.

'How long have you worked with horses?' Thierry asks, pulling his notebook out of his pocket. 'What other hidden secrets do you have?'

'More for your book?' Frederic grins.

Before Thierry can answer, the two almost collide with a boy madly waving a newspaper in front of their faces. It's Journal.

'Frederic!' he yells. 'You won't believe it! Thieves have stolen a rare pink diamond. It once belonged to Louis, Prince of Condé and it's worth twenty thousand francs!'

'Imagine having that much money,' says Frederic.

'I can't,' says Thierry. 'You could live on that for your entire life. Two lives! And have everything you want.'

Frederic and Thierry edge slowly past Journal on the narrow *passerelles*.

'See you round, Journal,' Frederic calls.

When the boys reach Frederic's home they are greeted by the balcony grannies still in their second floor apartment.

'There you are, boy!' one calls out, wrapped in a bundle of jackets and blankets and huddling under a large umbrella. 'We were wondering when you'd return.'

'And look! He has a friend!'

'Good lord, nothing says mischief like two boys!'

'Who are they?' Thierry whispers as they enter Frederic's apartment.

'The neighbourhood guards – nothing gets past them,' Frederic explains, before turning back to them and calling out: 'Do you need some food? I can bring some from the shelter for you!'

'Boys are always thinking with their stomachs!'

'That they are!'

'I'll take that as a no,' Frederic says to Thierry, laughing, as he pushes open the front door of the apartment. It takes a bit of effort against the force of the water – it has subsided a bit, but Frederic knows that he and his mother have a huge task ahead of them to make it liveable again when the water goes down.

'I miss my place,' says Thierry, looking around. He looks sad. 'I hope it's not completely underwater.'

'Do you want to go check on it?' Frederic suggests.

'Sure,' says Thierry. 'But *Maman* wants me to look in on her at work. After she heard about our sewer rescue yesterday, I think she wants to keep an eye on me.'

The boys lock the door behind them and head off to meet Thierry's mother.

On their way they pass a group of men, women and children gathered under an archway. They're obviously homeless, wearing tattered clothing, with old soggy blankets draped over their shoulders.

Frederic feels sorry for them. He's never really thought about the beggars in Paris before. They've always been there, but until the floods came they were kind of invisible, just like the pigeons. Everywhere, but part of the background.

Being homeless must be hard, he thinks. But being homeless in the winter in the middle of a flood would be brutal.

Then a girl standing at the edge of the group catches Frederic's eye. She turns and Frederic can't believe it.

It's Claire.

la bataille
THE FIGHT

Frederic chases after Thierry who is already on his way over to Claire.

'Out rescuing without us, eh?' Thierry says.

Claire looks startled and unhappy to see them.

'What are you doing? Following me?' she snaps, stepping away from the group and marching off.

The boys have to jog to keep up with her.

'No! Why would we be following you?' asks Frederic. 'We're on our way to meet Thierry's mother. Who were those people? Do you know them?'

'No! Sort of. Not really,' Claire says. 'Actually, I'm just helping those in need. Handing out some bread to the hungry. You know . . . that's what we do, right?'

It's obvious to Frederic that Claire is covering something up. He looks at Thierry, but he hasn't made the connection yet. She's either homeless or she knows someone who is, thinks Frederic.

He doesn't want to blow her cover. He knows what it's like to want to avoid talking about your miseries.

So he says nothing. She certainly looks flustered.

'Well, you should have taken us with you,' says Thierry. 'We can't be Fearless Frederic and the Flood-water Friends if one of us wants to go solo. *D'accord?* Anyway, do you want to come with us now?'

Claire shrugs.

When the three turn into the *rue de la Bûcherie* Frederic recognises it as the street his father took him to last summer to buy his kite.

And just a few moments later, as they approach the toy store, Frederic spots Monsieur Bertrand, the store owner.

He's with two men. As they get closer it's clear they're not friends. One steps forward and shoves Monsieur Bertrand. Despite his size, he stumbles.

'That doesn't look good!' says Claire.

'I think we should go another way and get the po-lice,' says Thierry. 'These guys look as if they mean business and someone could get seriously hurt . . .'

But before Thierry can finish his sentence, Frederic

bolts towards the shop.

When he splashes up alongside Monsieur Bertrand, the store-owner recognises him – the last time they saw each other was at Frederic's father's funeral.

'I could use your father right now, kid,' he says. 'Run and tell the police there are looters. You can't stay here. You'll get hurt. Go!'

But Frederic ignores Monsieur Bertrand and raises his clenched fists, ready to take on the robbers. He won't leave his side.

Two of the men laugh mockingly, as if Frederic's defiant stance is a joke to them. But then they lunge for Monsieur Bertrand and Frederic.

Frederic sidesteps a swing from one of the would-be robbers, thrusts his knee deep into the man's gut, and drives his elbow hard into his neck. The man is caught off guard and runs away, leaving his partner-in-crime to take on Monsieur Bertrand and Frederic alone.

But before the remaining robber can decide on his next move, his partner returns – this time with company. Three young thugs have joined him. Frederic recognises one of them – it's the pickpocket who stole the gentleman's watch! The one who threatened to make him pay.

The boy also seems to remember Frederic. He smirks.

Monsieur Bertrand and Frederic take a few wobbly steps back as the gang of robbers splash-walk through the water towards them.

'Police!' Monsieur Bertrand cries, his voice cracking with panic. 'Anyone! Help!'

Frederic turns to see that Claire is already running down the street to get help. Thierry, on the other hand, is standing a few steps away petrified.

Frederic knows he can defend himself with a punch or two and possibly even get a couple of bone-crunching kicks in, but with five against two the odds are against him and Monsieur Bertrand. No matter how skilled they are, there's no way they'll be able to overpower all five.

But suddenly, miraculously, another two figures turn into the street. Frederic can't believe his eyes! It's Monsieur Dupuis and the champion fighter Joseph.

It doesn't take them long to assess the situation, and they immediately rush to help.

Monsieur Dupuis starts swinging his walking stick with so much force that the sound of the cracks hitting the looters' backs reverberate down the street.

Within moments fists and feet are flying.

The pickpocket is the first to dive for Frederic,

but Frederic ducks and fires a one-two punch to the groin, swings around him and shoves him to the ground. The pickpocket falls head-first into the flooded street.

Frederic looks around him to check for more danger and sees Monsieur Bertrand grabbing one of the looters in an arm-hold. But with one swing he is knocked to the ground.

Monsieur Dupuis steps in to fend off the looter, and Joseph strikes two of the thugs at the same time with a double *coup de pied de figure* kick.

The pickpocket scrambles to his feet and clutches onto Frederic's coat – Frederic grabs the boy's hands. The two wrestle and sway from side to side, until Frederic headbutts the pickpocket on the chin.

The pickpocket releases his hold on Frederic and groans in pain, cupping his jaw. Frederic winds up his right arm ready to let loose with a direct punch, but he suddenly catches the pickpocket's expression.

He looks desperate and scared. And very young. In that moment Frederic realises that the pickpocket is probably homeless. Life for him is probably one long game of survival.

Frederic pulls back his punch. He lowers his fist as he hears the sound of police whistles approaching.

The pickpocket and the looters abruptly retreat,

sprinting as fast as they can in the opposite direction.

Then the police are in pursuit.

Frederic sees Claire running towards them. She pulls at Thierry's coat and drags him over to help Monsieur Bertrand to his feet. He catches his breath, and thanks them all for their courageous help.

'We heard you yelling,' says Joseph. 'There are gangs of looters and good-for-nothings making trouble all over town at the moment. Robbing houses that have be evacuated and making the most of the fact that the street-lights are out at night.'

Monsieur Dupuis nods. 'You should come to training, Frederic. You show so much potential, but you let that boy go! Come to the boxing hall one of these days. We haven't seen you there since your father . . .'

Joseph trails off.

Frederic answers with an awkward nod, and, in an attempt to change the subject, starts to introduce his friends. Claire steps forward and says hello. Thierry is once again writing manically into his notebook.

'Are you a journalist in the making?' says Joseph, grinning.

'No way!' says Thierry. 'I'm a novelist in the making. Now, that kick you did . . . What's the technical term for that?'

Claire grins. 'Come on, boys. We need to get going.'

'It's good to see you, Frederic,' calls Monsieur Bertrand.

Frederic waves, turns and chases after his friends.

'I can't believe it, Frederic! I just can't believe it!' Thierry says over and over as they approach the hotel where his mother works. 'You calm horses and you rumble like a sailor from Calais. Who are you?'

'What else are you hiding from us, Frederic?' says Claire as the three step up to the entrance of the Hotel Christophe-Antoine.

'Really?' Frederic says, raising his eyebrow at her. '*You're* asking me that question?'

But Claire doesn't answer. She just looks away.

l'hôtel
THE HOTEL

Frederic gasps as he steps into the grand lobby of the Hotel Christophe-Antoine. It's one of the few hotels in the city that has escaped the flooding. It's built on high foundations on one of the rare drier streets.

Inside, life goes on just as it did before the natural disaster hit. It's a completely different world, not at all like the bleak dreariness outside.

The lobby is warm and has electric lighting – the rest of the city has reverted to gas or wood fires. Frederic feels as though he hasn't been properly warm and dry in a long time.

The huge room has polished patterned wood floors, high ceilings with beams, windows with heavy embroidered drapes, and an imposing stone fireplace surrounded by couches and chairs.

Frederic soaks in the surroundings, but then he starts to notice the stares they're getting from the guests – women in large hats and full-length furs, men in top hats and tails, even children in coats with velvet collars.

He starts to feel self-conscious. Three grubby, damp children don't belong in such a luxurious place.

A hotel porter in a crimson uniform with gold buttons makes a hasty dash over the polished floor towards them.

'No loitering in here,' he snaps, waving his arms as if he's chasing away chickens. 'Out you go!'

'We're not loitering,' says Thierry. 'I'm here to see my *maman*, Marie Bonneville. She works here. She's a chambermaid.'

'Employees of this hotel enter in the laneway at the back,' the hotel porter says in an angry whisper. 'Didn't your *maman* tell you that? You must wait there. Now, please, you're dripping on the floor!'

'Oh, it's you!' comes a booming voice from behind them. 'I'm glad you found us. What luck!'

Frederic turns to see an elderly gentleman walking towards them.

At first Frederic doesn't recognise the man. He has an accent, bright rosy cheeks and smiling eyes.

He steps in front of the porter and shakes Frederic's hand. 'Lord Haythorne. I never forget a face.'

He calls over to a woman sitting in front of the fire. She's very beautiful and elegantly dressed. 'Darling, this is the boy I told you about.'

'Oh, yes, yes, *oui, oui!*' She beams. 'My husband has not stopped talking about you. This watch has been in the family a century. It means more to him than all our homes in England.'

Ah! Frederic remembers him now. And that explains the accent. They are English aristocrats from across the channel.

'How many homes do you have?' Thierry blurts out, only to get a jab in the ribs by Claire.

The man waves the porter away. 'This boy and his friends are my guests today. He helped me and then ran off without accepting a reward.'

The porter nods and Claire cheekily pokes her tongue out at him.

'Oh, James,' sighs his wife. 'Look at them in their dirty wet clothes. It's all so grimy and drab. They look like stray hungry kittens. Let's buy them some warm new clothes and then have pastries and hot chocolate together.'

'What a smashing idea!' Lord Haythorne declares in English.

'What's your name, dear?' his wife says to Claire.

'Claire.'

'Oh!' says Lady Haythorne excitedly. 'We share the same name.'

Thierry looks delighted and scribbles madly in his notebook. 'Smeshion aydeer-err!' he says, trying to copy Lord Haythorne's English.

Everyone laughs. Even Frederic is smiling.

A half hour later, Frederic and Thierry are kitted out in new pants, boots, vests, jackets and caps. Frederic feels different – in a good way. He feels strangely taller. The new clothes hug him like another skin and make him want to stand up very straight. As for his new knee-high leather boots – he can't wait to splash through the water in them.

The boys are ushered into the hotel restaurant by the porter. They timidly head over to join Lord Haythorne, who has his head buried in a newspaper. Frederic notices that the headlines on the front page continue to be about the flood and the diamond robbery that *Journal* mentioned.

'Now, that's more like it,' Lord Haythorne says. 'Fine young gentlemen. We'll wait for the girls to arrive before we order, *d'accord*?'

Frederic and Thierry exchange grins, savouring the moment.

'My stars!' Thierry gasps.

Frederic follows his gaze and sees Lady Haythorne entering the restaurant with a young lady wearing a peach-coloured dress with a lace collar and sleeves. She has ribbons and flowers in her hair.

'Where's Claire?' Frederic asks Thierry.

Thierry laughs. 'That *is* Claire,' he says.

Frederic almost can't believe it. 'Wow! Claire is beautiful! I mean really beautiful!'

Claire takes a seat between Thierry and Frederic.

'You smell like lilacs,' Thierry says.

'Shut up!' Claire hisses. 'And what are you staring at, Frederic?'

'Um, nothing, I wasn't staring . . . Sorry, Claire. It's just that you look so different.'

Lord and Lady Haythorne order rich, dark hot chocolate and a selection of the hotel's finest pastries: creamy *éclairs*, an upside-down *tarte Tatin* with caramelised apples smothered in sugar and butter, and the hotel's specialty, the *mille-feuille*, a custard slice made up of layers and layers of delicate puff pastry and cream, dusted with icing sugar and roasted almonds.

'I think this is the greatest thing that's ever happened to me,' says Thierry. He cradles his cup of chocolate near his chin.

Claire and Frederic just scoff down the delicacies in silent bliss. There is no time to talk when you're surrounded by the most delicious treats in the world – though Thierry does manage to tell the Haythornes, in between bites, how the three of them have become friends because of the flood.

When the sweet feast is over, Lady Haythorne asks Claire if she would come with her. She is going to meet with a French women's group.

'We come together once a month to discuss the rights of women,' she says. 'We are making great strides in fighting for equality for women – in sports, politics, in life in general. I mean, why should the boys have all the fun? Will you join me?'

Claire nods and grins widely.

'Enjoy yourself, my love,' says Lord Haythorne. 'That will give me a chance to catch up on some paperwork. Boys, when you're ready, I'll have the porter arrange a carriage to take you back to your shelter.'

As Claire and Lady Haythorne leave, Frederic catches Claire looking back at them. She looks genuinely happy.

'Oh no!' Thierry says, standing up from the table.

'*Maman*! I forgot all about her! I'll see you at the shelter, Frederic. And, thank you, Monsieur Haythorne.' Thierry bolts out of the restaurant.

'No need to rush, Frederic,' says Lord Haythorne, standing. 'Finish your hot chocolate. I wish you and your friends all the best.'

Frederic watches Lord Haythorne leave. He sighs contentedly but as he's about to take another sip from his cup, his eyes fall on a figure entering the dining room. Frederic almost chokes on his chocolate.

It's the thief from the Louvre.

se cacher
HIDING

Frederic snatches up the newspaper on the table and hides his face behind it. He cautiously peers over the top and tracks the man as he walks over to a waiter at the far end of the restaurant.

He is dressed differently now – a lot smarter, in a tailored jacket. He doesn't seem to be hiding or be concerned that he might be seen. The man and the waiter chat briefly and then he leaves.

Frederic jumps from the table and follows him.

The man makes his way to the back of the lobby and up a grand spiral stairway. Frederic is careful to keep a safe distance between them. At the top, the man turns the corner into a long corridor.

Frederic leans against the wall at the top of the stairway and peers around the corner. He sees the man unlocking the door to room 22. Then he disappears inside.

Frederic's hands are shaking and his mouth is dry. He walks towards the room until there is just a single door between him and the man who murdered his father.

A wave of blazing anger washes over Frederic. He clenches his fist and grits his teeth. And just as he is about to rap at the door, he hears voices coming up the stairway.

There is a chambermaid's cart in the middle of the corridor a few doors down, filled with fresh towels and sheets. He runs and huddles behind the large metal trolley. The voices of two men echo along the passageway. He hears a knock and peeks from behind the trolley. They're at the man's door!

Frederic wonders if they are the accomplices from the night at the Louvre museum. They had masks on so it's hard to know. One is short, balding and has a moustache, like most men in Paris. The other is tall, thin and has a goatee beard. The door opens slowly.

'Finally!' says the man. 'I went down to the restaurant to see if you were there. What took you so long?'

The man speaks with an accent that suggests he is

educated and from the upper class.

'You can blame this damn flood! It takes twice as long to get anywhere,' says one of the men in a rough accent more like Frederic's.

'This isn't a bad place to lay low for a couple of nights,' says the other. 'And you'll be happy to know all is set to go. Another guard in place ready for Friday night and we'll soon be smiling with her . . .'

'*Shhh!* Come in!'

The door slams and Frederic exhales.

'What do you think you're doing?' A voice comes from behind Frederic.

Frederic jumps. He turns to see a chambermaid scowling at him. He knows he shouldn't be in this part of the hotel. He's certain he'll be reported.

But the woman's scowl turns to a curious half smile instead. 'Frederic? Thierry's friend, from the shelter?' she says. 'But what are you doing up here?'

'Um, I was . . . looking for Thierry.' Frederic lies, recognising Thierry's mother.

'Well, I was just with him down in the maids' quarters. I understand you all had an unexpected shopping expedition – thanks to you, apparently. At least there was no jumping into sewers or rescuing cats from crocodiles. Thierry is on his way back to the shelter.'

Thierry's mother opens a side panel on the cart to reveal room keys dangling off small hooks. She hangs a key, takes another, and grabs a cloth from the top of the trolley.

Frederic has an idea. There's no time to think about the consequences, about how dangerous it is or how much trouble he might get himself or Thierry's mother into.

'I'll see if I can catch up with him,' says Frederic, pretending to say goodbye.

As Thierry's mother steps into another room, Frederic opens the side panel on the cart and snatches the key to room number 22.

le loup
THE WOLF

Frederic doesn't sleep much that night. And when he wakes up the following morning his mother notices the anxious look on his face.

'You were tossing and turning all night,' she says, already dressed to leave for the day. 'Is there anything you want to tell me? Perhaps I can help.'

Frederic is torn. He wants to tell his mother everything – that he knows where to find his father's murderer, that he has a plan to get revenge. But his mother will just tell him to go to the police. And he knows how much help that was last time.

'You always worry, but there's no need,' he says, hugging her goodbye.

After she leaves, Frederic sneaks out of the shelter before Thierry and Claire see him. The streets are once again drizzly and grey. He wonders if the rain and the flood will ever go away.

He walks quickly along the *passerelles* back to the Hotel Christophe-Antoine. Once there, Frederic positions himself directly across the road from the hotel, behind a street vendor selling roasted chestnuts. They smell so good, he thinks, his stomach grumbling.

Frederic waits.

And waits. And waits.

A long hour later he spots his father's killer stepping out of the hotel. The man hails a taxi-carriage and rides off.

'Now!' Frederic whispers under his breath, splashing across the street and entering the hotel at the main entrance.

'Where do you think you're going?'

Frederic is startled – it's the same porter from yesterday and despite Frederic's fancy new clothes he knows he doesn't belong.

'I was asked to meet Lord Haythorne,' Frederic lies.

'Really?' says the porter, his eyes narrowing with suspicion.

'Yes, and I'm running late,' adds Frederic. 'I don't

think Lord Haythorne would appreciate your holding me up. Between you and me, he told me he wasn't really happy with your service and was thinking of reporting you to the manager. If you let me pass perhaps I might be able to put in a good word for you.'

The porter looks a bit worried. Finally he steps back and waves Frederic through.

When Frederic reaches room 22, he takes a deep breath. It's the riskiest thing he's ever done. He's gambling on the other two men not being here. He listens. Nothing. Then he lets himself in.

Frederic wastes no time. There's a bag on the bed, and clothes neatly hung up in the wardrobe and placed in the drawers. It's all very neat and orderly, not at all what Frederic was expecting.

Somehow he thought that the man who killed his father would be grubby and messy, out of control somehow. But this man is a gentleman. He fits right in here. A wolf in sheep's clothing.

Frederic rummages through the bag. He is looking for more information about who this man is, something that will help him get revenge.

Then on the desk, he finds a letter from the hotel addressed to their guest: *Dear Monsieur Manteau* . . . it reads. He quickly scans the letter, but it's nothing out of the ordinary.

Still, he has a name, even if it's not real.

'Manteau,' Frederic mutters.

Suddenly the doorknob rattles.

poursuivi
FOLLOWED

Frederic throws himself to the ground and rolls under the bed just as the door swings open.

His heart is pounding. Are the two men from yesterday here? Is Manteau back so soon? Frederic hears the sound of two voices.

'Maybe we misjudged,' says one. 'Perhaps he's in the room next door.'

'Then why is this one open?' says the other voice.

Frederic lets out a huge sigh of relief and crawls out from under the bed.

'What are you doing here?' he asks, startling Thierry and Claire. 'Did you follow me?'

'Of course we followed you,' says Claire. 'And we

watched you watching the hotel. What do you think you're doing?'

Frederic sighs, wishing he had been careful to lock the door behind him. 'It's got nothing to do with you two and it isn't safe for you to be here.'

'Why? Whose room are we in?' asks Thierry.

Frederic doesn't answer, but he doesn't have to because Claire answers for him.

'If I'm right, and I always am, then it isn't safe for any of us to be here. I think we're in the room of the man Frederic saw on the street, the one he thinks killed his father.' Claire shakes her head at Frederic. 'Are you crazy?'

'What? *Ce n'est pas possible!* It's not possible!' Thierry sounds panicked now. 'Let's go to the police. Tell the hotel manager . . . Tell someone!'

'No!' Frederic snaps. 'We're not telling anyone. Not yet.'

'Why? Because you want to confront him? Let him have it?' asks Claire.

'Maybe I do. I don't know. It's just . . .' Frederic feels agitated and lost. And starving. He starts pacing around the room, grabs an apple from the fruit bowl on the desk and bites into it.

A shooting pain goes through his jaw. The apple is hard as rock. He puts his hand to his mouth. 'I almost chipped my tooth. What's in here?'

Frederic splits open the apple.

Something glints from inside the white fruit.

'*Oh la vache*, holy cow!' gasps Claire. 'Is it a jewel?'

'That's the stolen Prince of Condé diamond,' cries Thierry. 'The same one in the newspaper! The one that boy said was worth twenty thousand francs.'

'Twenty thousand!' says Claire. 'I'm sure there's a huge reward out for this.'

'It's like something from an Émile Gaboriau or a Sherlock Holmes detective novel,' says Thierry. 'If we go to the police now and return the diamond to the authorities, they will catch your father's killer and put him away for life.'

Frederic stares down at the diamond – it's a light-pink pear-shaped stone.

'I've got a better plan,' he says. He grabs Thierry's notebook and pencil and rips out a page.

If you want the diamond back, meet me at midnight at the Charlemagne statue in front of the Notre Dame Cathedral, Frederic writes. *Come alone.*

perdu
LOST

'I can't let you do this,' Claire whispers. 'I'm sorry about your father – we've all lost our fathers. But this isn't some fantasy world like in one of the books Thierry reads. You're putting yourself in danger . . . and for what? You'll wind up dead.'

'*Exactement!* Exactly!' Thierry adds. 'I don't know what you think you'll do when you meet this man, but it can't end well. Please, Frederic. Can't we just go back to saving cats from crocodiles?'

'I'm going to tell someone,' declares Claire.

Thierry nods.

Frederic feels his eyes beginning to sting and struggles to keep his tears at bay. They should be with me, he thinks. These are my friends. His breath quickens and his stomach churns. Why are they against me?

'I wouldn't be so quick to tell anyone, Thierry,' he hisses. 'Because I'll tell the hotel manager that I got the room key from your mother and she will probably lose her job.'

'You wouldn't!' says Thierry.

'I would!' Frederic tells him.

'And if you tell, Claire,' Frederic says. 'I'll tell the nuns at the shelter that you're just a regular homeless person, not a flood victim. You shouldn't be at the shelter – it's for people with families and places to live. They don't let the beggars in.'

Claire stares at him, shocked.

'That's right, I know! You think I couldn't work it out. You're homeless. An orphan. This flood must be the best thing that's happened to you – all that free food and board.'

The spiteful words have just flown out of Frederic's mouth and instantly he regrets what he's said, but it's too late to take them back.

Thierry grabs his notebook and runs out the door.

Claire goes to follow him, but before she does she turns back to face Frederic.

'You're right, of course,' she says, her voice cracking. 'This flood *was* the best thing that ever happened to me, but it wasn't the free food or the roof over my head. It was you two. For the first time, I thought I had friends.'

She closes the door behind her, leaving Frederic feeling like the worst person in the world.

Probably because I am, he thinks.

—

Later that night at the shelter Frederic is especially grateful for the warmth of the heaters as he weaves past the other evacuees. There are more displaced families in the church hall than on the previous nights. It's packed.

Frederic scans the room for Claire. She's nowhere to be seen. He wonders miserably where she could be. Where she will be sleeping tonight. In an abandoned train carriage or a junkyard shed? Or huddled in blankets and newspapers under an archway or bridge somewhere?

Frederic sighs and looks for Thierry.

But when Frederic reaches the spot where Thierry and his mother have been camped, he sees another woman and her children have taken their place.

'Where's Thierry and his *maman*?' Frederic asks the woman nursing her baby.

'The people here before us?' she asks.

Frederic nods.

'They left. The flooding on their street has subsided. They've gone home.'

Frederic thanks her. He doesn't even know where Thierry lives. And just like that, his only friends are gone.

Frederic feels filled with grief and loneliness. He hasn't felt this lost since the night his father died.

He puts his hand in the pocket of his jacket and feels the cold hard diamond there.

This time tomorrow night he'll face his father's killer and now he has nothing to lose.

revers fouetté
REVERSE ROUNDHOUSE KICK

The time has arrived. It's time to confront Manteau.

Frederic pushes the diamond into a sock and hides it in his luggage. Whatever happens, Manteau won't walk away with the prize.

He quietly tiptoes away from his sleeping mother and steps out of the hall into the dark, freezing city.

Frederic runs as fast as he can into the night. He runs to keep warm, but also to stop himself from reconsidering and returning to the shelter. For the first time in a long time there are hardly any clouds in the sky, and the flooded streets shimmer in the light of the full moon and from the electric street lamps that have been reinstalled with gas lighting.

He jumps from *passerelles* to *passerelles*, street to street. He darts over the bridge of *Louis-Philippe*, then across the smaller and narrower *Pont Saint-Louis* and ends up directly behind Notre Dame.

Frederic stops and catches his breath and takes in the silhouette of the cathedral looming over him. Making a sharp left he stands at the entrance, then races towards the giant bronze figure of King Charlemagne perched on his horse.

It's so eerily silent that Frederic can hear the rushing current of the river and his own heart beating rapidly against his chest. But then he hears a slight scraping behind him. He whips his head back towards the cathedral.

No one. Not a soul in sight.

He tells himself he mustn't let his nerves get the better of him. But when he turns to face King Charlemagne he is startled to see a figure emerge from behind the statue.

It's the man called Manteau.

For a moment, Frederic stops breathing and his legs feel wobbly and weak. He exhales.

'A boy?' Manteau hisses, before breaking into a coughing chuckle. 'What game is this? Who has put you up to this?'

'This isn't a game!' Frederic stutters, feeling his

courage return. 'I'm here to make you pay for what you did to my father.'

With only a few metres between them, Manteau takes another step closer to Frederic. He looks confused.

With a rush of anger Frederic realises that he doesn't recognise him.

'You don't remember me or my father, do you?'

Manteau laughs again. 'Can't say that I do. Should I?' As the clouds move across the moon, the light reveals more clearly his stone-cold face.

How could he forget? wonders Frederic. Wouldn't killing a man remain as clear as day? Is killing people such a normal event for this hateful murderer? He feels desperate for this man to say something, anything about his father, to show the slightest bit of remorse. To admit what he's done.

'You killed him!' Frederic says.

He's overcome with so much fury that all he wants to do is to charge at Manteau. But he doesn't.

'The Louvre! Last summer!' he spits.

'Oh,' the man says. Then he shrugs his shoulders. 'And? So what? He got in the way of my business. I guess it was a bit of bad luck for him, eh?'

'A bit of bad luck?' says Frederic. He feels his fists clench.

'Enough of your foolishness, boy. Give me the diamond,' Manteau demands. 'Or you'll end up in the same place as your papa. Come on, hand it over.' He steps closer to Frederic and pulls something from his coat. He holds it up and Frederic can see that it's a dagger.

'Boy, if you've come to teach me a lesson, you're making a mistake. I don't take lessons. Now . . . I'll ask you one more time, where is the diamond?'

'I don't have it!' Frederic snaps defiantly. 'You don't actually think I'd bring it with me, do you?'

Manteau's eyes narrow and his top lip curls. He glares at Frederic for a moment, turns and begins to walk away.

'What are you doing?' Frederic calls. He feels himself becoming increasingly agitated. He expected many things, but not this.

'Hey!' he calls after Manteau. 'Where are you going?'

'You've wasted my time, boy,' he says, without turning. 'There are plenty of other jewels to rob, plenty more art that I will get a very good price for.'

Frederic is taken aback. Is this evil man just going to walk away? As if this was nothing? As if his father's life meant nothing?

'That's it?' Frederic shouts. He can feel the emotion welling up inside him and he can't hold it in. He chokes on a sob and he can hear the tears in his voice. 'Are you really going to walk off like some coward?'

Manteau does not answer Frederic. As he slips away into the night, two other figures emerge from the darkness. It's the two men who had showed up at the hotel room. Frederic contemplates turning and making a run for it, but he tells himself he must stand his ground this time, for his father. He brushes away the tears, clenches his fists and widens his stance.

The tall one rushes at him first with a dagger.

Frederic sidesteps him, and let's loose with a *coup de pied au corp*, a forward kick to the body – but his foot is knocked away before making contact.

Frederic is caught off guard.

The tall man lunges at him again, and Frederic ducks, grabs the hand holding the dagger and bites hard into it. The man growls and drops his weapon. Frederic follows up with a knee-thrust into his ribs.

The man grimaces and throws an unexpected left punch into Frederic's neck.

Frederic stumbles backward, doubling over and clasping at his throat. He coughs and gasps – and isn't prepared for the shorter man who follows up with a *revers fouetté* – a reverse roundhouse kick – into Frederic's hip.

Frederic is knocked off his feet and hits the flooded ground hard with a splash. The bitterly cold water startles him, but before he can get back up on his feet, the two men jump on top of him. He gasps at a lungful of air before he feels his face pushed under the water.

Frederic wriggles and struggles to shove the men off – but they're too heavy. He sees bubbles of air rapidly leaving his mouth and tries not to breathe in water.

He's so dizzy now, he's about to pass out.

Just before he does, the two men yank him back out of the water.

Frederic gasps, coughs and splutters, sucking in as much oxygen as he can. The short one frisks him, rummaging through his pockets.

'He doesn't have the diamond on him,' he growls.

'Don't think this is over, boy,' snarls the other, before letting loose with a forceful backhanded slap across Frederic's face.

Frederic topples backwards, his face once again submerged underwater.

For a moment Frederic lies motionless, finally realising that no one is holding him down, that the men have gone.

What a fool to think that confronting my father's

killer would solve anything, he thinks. I'll never get remorse from Manteau. And I'll never be the son my father wanted.

encore ensemble
TOGETHER AGAIN

Frederic drags himself back to the shelter, soaking wet, limping and sore, constantly checking that he isn't being followed. For the first time he lets himself think about how things could have been different without that terrible night in the museum.

Would I have told my father what I wanted? he wonders. I never told him about the horses or that I didn't want to be a fighter. Would I have had the courage to go my own way?

I hope so. One day.

Suddenly he realises what he needs to do.

If I'm to beat Manteau, I'll have to do it my way, he thinks. And I can't do it alone.

He only hopes his friends will forgive him.

Frederic runs non-stop all the way back to the shelter with a new plan in mind.

—

The following morning when Frederic wakes, his entire body hurts. The right side of his face throbs and feels twice the size. He touches under his eye and feels how swollen it is. He looks down at his hip and chest – they are deep red with spreading bruises.

He quickly rolls over to hide his face when he hears his mother stirring. He pretends to be sleeping.

'Be good,' she whispers into his ear, and kisses him on the top of his head. 'I'm off to work.'

Frederic moans as if he is just waking up and waits until she's made her way out of the shelter. He then hastily shuffles over to the closest heating station where he has left his wet clothes to dry overnight.

A minute later, he is back in the cold streets and is walking as fast as he can towards the Left Bank of the city to find Claire.

When he reaches the junkyard, where they found the rowboat, he hopes his hunch is correct. He steps into the old train carriage and is surprised to see an entire family huddled together under blankets.

'What do you want?' says the father.

'I'm so sorry,' says Frederic. 'I'm looking for Claire.'

'Who?' asks the mother, cradling a toddler.

'I know Claire,' says an older child, about Frederic's age. 'I think she sometimes sleeps in the other carriage, at the top of the junkyard. But I haven't seen her recently.'

'Thanks,' says Frederic, rushing out.

When Frederic steps into the other abandoned carriage he sees Claire lying on the floor fast asleep next to another family.

He coughs loudly.

They all look up startled.

Claire springs up. She looks shocked to see him. 'What are you doing here?' she says, sounding angry.

'Who is he?' asks the woman beside her.

'Just someone I know. He's not dangerous. Go back to sleep,' Claire says, standing up and dragging Frederic outside.

He notices that she is wearing her usual dress and jacket but has kept her new boots. He wonders if she has sold the new clothes for food.

'I wanted to find you,' says Frederic. 'Was that your mother?'

'No,' says Claire. 'You think you know everything, but you don't. I never knew my father and my mother died of pneumonia two years ago. These people have looked after me since then – and better than any orphanage would have.'

Frederic sighs. 'I'm sorry.'

'I don't need your pity. I'm fine as I am. At least I'm free.'

'No,' says Frederic. 'That's not what I meant. I'm sorry I said those things. Without those shelters we would *all* be homeless. And you were right – I was so wrong to think I'd be able to take on my father's killer on my own. I can't. So I'm here to ask your help, even though I don't deserve it. Please, Claire. Will you help me?'

Claire screws up her face, and doesn't answer.

'To be honest, you and Thierry were the best things that happened to me too,' says Frederic.

Slowly, Claire's scowl turns into a grin. She nods. 'Of course I'll help you,' she says. 'You always help your friends.'

She reaches out her hand to shake his.

'I need Thierry's help too,' Frederic says, taking her hand. 'I need the three of us – the Floodwater Friends or Terrific Trio or the Crocodile Crusaders or whatever he wants to call us! But I don't know where he lives.'

'It doesn't matter where he lives,' says Claire.

'Where else would Thierry be if he's not at home?'

Frederic thinks for a moment and recalls Thierry saying the place where he reads most of his books.

'The Sainte Genevieve library!'

Claire nods.

'We'd better get going,' Frederic says. 'Because once we find Thierry we've got a lot to do.'

pas d'enfants!
NO CHILDREN!

As he steps into the foyer of the Sainte Genevieve library, Frederic feels as out of place as he did in the lobby of the Hotel Christophe-Antoine. But it's a very different place – there is nothing soft and plush and warm here. Cold stone columns hold up an impossibly high roof and the large tiled floor is bare of rugs. It's more like a government building than a place to find books. Directly in front of them, a huge stone stairway leads upwards.

He notices Claire straightening up and brushing down her dress – even she looks intimidated.

'He must be in the reading room and those stairs are the only way in,' Frederic says to her. 'Let's go.'

The two walk towards the stairs and two men coming down glare with disapproval.

At the top of the stairs is a massive door. Behind it, Frederic feels sure, are all the books Thierry has spoken about . . . and Thierry.

But a man steps between them and the door. He's pencil-thin and scowling, with his lips pursed tightly. He's wearing a guard's uniform.

'No children are allowed!' he says. 'Shoo!'

'But that can't be right,' Claire says. 'Our friend says he reads here. And he's only twelve.'

The man shakes his head. 'No one under the age of eighteen is allowed in the library – and even then they have to be registered. Come back in about six years. In the meantime, I insist you leave!'

'But how does Thierry get in?' Claire asks Frederic.

The guard rolls his eyes. 'Oh, Thierry Bonneville,' he sneers. 'Well, if I had it my way he wouldn't. But he has a job – the tedious chore of dusting the spines of the books. Instead of being paid, he is allowed to read. But he is the exception. No other *enfants* are allowed.'

'Well, if we're not allowed in, could you please let him know we're here to see him?' Frederic asks as politely as possible.

'Who do you think I am? No. I will not retrieve

your friend as if I'm some hunting dog. Now . . . leave!'

Claire pulls at Frederic's sleeve and turns to head back down the stairs.

'I'm going to distract the guard,' she whispers to Frederic. 'And you run in . . . *d'accord*? Just let me know when he turns his back to us.'

Frederic glances over his shoulder to see the guard turning away. Just as the man opens the door to step into the reading room, Frederic hears a scream.

He whips his head around to see Claire sprawled out on the ground at the bottom of the stairs. For a moment even he's worried – it looks frighteningly believable. She's a good actress, he thinks.

'Help! Help!' he cries, running down to be by her side.

The guard rushes down the stairs right behind him.

'What happened?' he cries. 'Is she breathing?'

Claire is motionless, pretending to be out cold.

'I think you should try to feel for her pulse . . . or raise her head. I'll go try to find someone to help,' says Frederic. He backs away and sprints up the stairs.

He races through the doorway and is stopped in his tracks by what he finds.

He never expected a library to be so grand and monumental. The dizzyingly high ceiling, shaped like half-barrels, sits above enormous arched windows. This one room is almost as large and tall as a grand train station. Two storeys of books line the walls. Running through the middle of the room are rows and rows of tables, filled with people hunched over books.

But it's deathly quiet. Frederic can't believe that a room full of so many people can be so silent.

Thierry is nowhere to be seen. How will I ever find him in this huge space? Frederic wonders.

Another guard has already spotted him and is marching towards him. Frederic walks at a clipped pace in the opposite direction, frantically scanning the tables and the people standing at the bookshelves and the balcony walkways of the second level.

People lift their heads and frown at Frederic.

'What are you doing here?' a man says.

People whisper and mutter. 'What's the meaning of this?'

'Who's that?'

And then the guard who had been attending to Claire bursts through the doors.

'Get that boy!' he calls.

Frederic makes a run for it – dodging and weaving

around the rows of tables and scanning for Thierry at the same time.

'Thierry!' he shouts. 'Thierry Bonneville! Are you here? I'm sorry about what I said to you! I was heartless and cruel, and I shouldn't have said those things to a friend like you. You and Claire are the best friends I've ever had.'

People in the library try to shush Frederic angrily.

'*Shhh!*' they hiss. '*Shhhhh!*'

'This is a library! Not a fish market!'

'How dare you!'

'Thierry!' Frederic calls again. 'Please! I need your help. I need the Floodwater Friends to come together just one more time.'

And then, at the very far end of the library, Frederic spots a familiar face in the sea of seated readers.

Thierry stands up. 'Frederic!' he calls excitedly. 'Of course I'll help you! This is just like in *The Three Musketeers*. All for one and one for all! United we stand, divided we fall!'

La Joconde
MONA LISA

There's a spooky stillness in the dark, grand hallways of the Louvre Museum. The characters in the paintings stare into the blackness as if on guard. But there's movement coming from the Salon Carré gallery.

Footsteps enter the hall and two dim hand-held lanterns move across the room as if floating.

'Here she is,' whispers a male voice with an upper-class accent.

The light in the lantern flares, brightening the masked faces of three men and the painting of *La Joconde*. She looks out at the three men.

A guard in full uniform stands by the door. 'I'll leave you three to it,' he says. 'I figure you have ten minutes, tops. You and your men must act quickly.'

The footsteps of the guard echo as he hurriedly leaves the salon.

'Right, Roux, take the lamp,' says Manteau, his hands already clasping the frame.

'Do you think she's smiling, Etienne?' Roux asks the third, taller man.

'Who cares!' snaps Manteau. 'Now hold that lamp still!'

'I still think she looks hungry,' comes another, younger voice from the corner of the gallery.

Manteau and his men seem startled. They turn their lamps in the direction of the voice.

une leçon
A LESSON

Frederic emerges from the darkness.

'You!' says the short man.

'Perhaps we should've drowned him when we had the chance,' says the tall man.

'You have some nerve, boy,' snarls Manteau. 'Why are you here? How?'

Frederic shrugs. 'I overheard these two saying that they've got another guard ready for Friday night and that soon you'll be "smiling with her". It would have meant nothing to someone else, but when I thought about it I realised I knew exactly what it meant. You obviously have another guard working for you and *La Joconde* is the most famous smiling woman I know.'

Manteau claps slowly.

'Bravo,' he hisses. 'You have all the makings of a detective. But we've also been doing a little investigating. After this we're going to pay the Saint Nicholas shelter a visit and collect our diamond. But now you've at least saved us the effort of killing you there.'

Manteau cracks his knuckles.

'Have you come here to cry about your father again? To teach me another lesson for killing him? To fight?' asks Manteau, now slowly walking towards Frederic. 'Because I think that the one who will be taught a lesson . . . is you.'

'I'm not going to fight you,' Frederic says. He feels calm and determined. 'I'm no longer going to fight or blame myself for my father's death. And I've already learnt my lesson so I've called on some help. Because that's what you do when you're in trouble – good people will help.'

He turns to see Claire and Thierry stepping out of the shadows.

'What is this? A school trip?' Manteau scoffs.

But Roux and Etienne have started to look nervous behind him.

'These are my friends,' says Frederic proudly. 'And now you've admitted to your crimes, they're here to lock you three away for good.'

'These children?' growls Manteau. 'Pathetic!'

'No,' says Claire.

'Not us,' says Thierry.

Then Manteau follows Frederic's gaze to the door.

Stepping into the salon is Officer Pierre and a troop of a dozen policemen. Behind them are Monsieur Dupuis, Joseph and the men from the boxing hall.

'Arrest them!' Officer Pierre orders his troop of men.

Faced with this, Manteau and his accomplices are apprehended without a fight.

'I cannot believe this,' Manteau hisses at Frederic as he's dragged out of the room. 'Captured by some boy! A nobody!'

'He's not nobody,' says Thierry. 'He's Fearless Frederic!'

'Fearless Frederic and his Floodwater Friends,' Claire says, taking Frederic's and Thierry's hands and squeezing them tightly. 'And don't you forget it!'

fin
THE END

In the Tuileries Gardens, Frederic holds tightly on to the bridle of the kite and runs as fast as he can in the direction of the Louvre.

Picking up speed, with the warm spring wind blowing across his face, he lets the line out and the Eagle whooshes up into the bright blue sky.

Frederic stops, turns his back to the wind and continues to evenly release the string. Higher and higher the kite flies, and Frederic beams from ear to ear.

A crowd gathers to watch, and then Thierry bursts through the gathering.

'Wow! You're doing it! You're actually flying it!' he says excitedly.

'You're late. What took you so long?' Frederic asks, his eyes still on the kite.

'I've almost finished writing my book,' Thierry says enthusiastically, taking out his notebook. 'Listen, what do you think?

'*It was not the last time they would heed this lesson to call on their friends. The balcony grannies offered to share their apartment with Frederic and his maman until the water subsided and the city of Paris returned to its beautiful self. Frederic went back to work with his beloved horses and, even though he lost his job at the library, Thierry was offered real work in the bookstore with Monsieur and Madame Martin when he finishes school.*

'*What followed after that was a series of fortunate events. A large sum of money was offered for the return of the rare Prince of Condé diamond – shared equally with Fearless Frederic and the Floodwater Friends. Frederic's and Thierry's mothers were able to rebuild their homes after the devastation of the flood.*

'*Claire shared her portion among the people who had cared for her and she was taken in at an orphanage. But she wasn't there for long. When Frederic let the Haythornes know of her circumstances, they adopted her and she has moved to England as the daughter they always wanted.*'

'Sounds good,' says Frederic, but he can't help

thinking about the young pickpocket. He hasn't seen him since their fight and he hopes the boy's story has turned out well too. He knows, however, that for most homeless people the story has been very different.

'It's almost too good to be true, isn't it, Thierry?' he says. 'You've just reminded me, pull out the letter in my pocket. It's from Claire.'

Thierry snatches the envelope from Frederic's jacket and opens it.

'*Dear Hero*,' he reads aloud. '*As you can see, my writing is improving. I can now write in French and one day I will be able to write in English. Not bad! Although, Maman is helping me a little with this letter. This is just a short note to say that we will be visiting Paris next month and staying for the summer. Isn't that wonderful? So get the Eagle out and we will fly it together – although you've probably flown it a few times by now and Thierry has probably written an entire instructional booklet about kite-flying. Give him a big hug from me. I can't wait to see you both. Love Claire.*'

'An instructional booklet is a great idea,' says Thierry.

'I thought you'd say that.' Frederic smiles. 'Here. You can have a try.'

As Frederic hands the kite over to his friend he hears a familiar voice.

'Halley's comet perilously close to Earth! Some say it was the cause of the flood and now it could mean the end of the world is coming!'

It's Journal. He spots Frederic, throws his bag of papers over his shoulder and saunters over to them.

'Is that your kite?' he asks.

Frederic nods.

'I've never seen one in real life before. It's a beauty!'

'So is that headline true, Journal?' Frederic asks.

'I don't know.' He shrugs. 'I didn't really believe that men could fly, but they can. Some news is real. Some news is false. Right now in Paris, anything feels possible.'

'Well, if the world really is going to come to an end I better go and do the thing I really love,' says Frederic walking away. 'Boss Gustave said that he might break his rule one day about riding the carriage horses. Maybe today is the day.'

'But what about your kite?' Thierry calls out.

'You and Journal have fun with it. Just return it to me later.'

'*Merci beaucoup!*' yells Thierry. 'Say hello to Charlemagne for me.'

'I will,' says Frederic, smiling and looking up at the Louvre museum across the gardens. 'I will.'

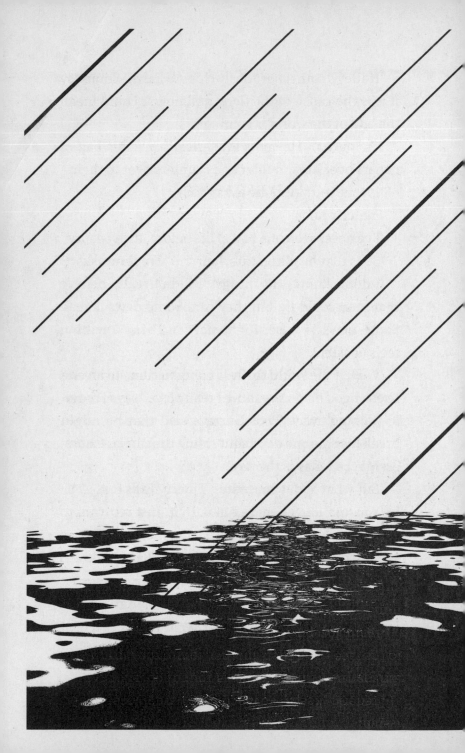

FROM THE AUTHOR

My first introduction to France was when I was in high school. I took Year 10 French, and I loved it, mostly because of my teacher, Mr Franzoni, who was so enthusiastic and engaging. He made France, especially Paris, sound like the most magical place on earth. I promised myself that one day I would visit the City of Lights.

A few years later, I was working as an actor on a popular TV show. I couldn't believe my luck when I was invited to do a photo shoot in Paris for a teen magazine. Along with other young actors and models we raced around all the major landmarks of the city with the photographer. But all I wanted to do was to break away and explore the amazing city that I was only getting glimpses of.

Since then I've been fortunate enough to visit Paris six times, but I still haven't seen it all. In July 2016, the city was experiencing major flooding – the Seine River had risen higher than it had for years. I overheard locals make reference to another flood in Paris's history – they called it 'the Great Flood'.

When I looked it up, incredible black-and-white photographs of the flood of 1910 came up on the screen. The images of Parisians shuffling along gangplanks or rowing boats down famous boulevards are so evocative, so poignant.

But the flood didn't come rushing down the river. The water rose up from the ground, from the sewers and the drains until the city was covered.

I started wondering, what would it have been like to wake up to discover your home was underwater? What were the shelters like in 1910? How did people help one another when faced with a catastrophe? Who were the heroes and the villains?

I wondered, if I were a kid in the shelters, how would I feel? Would I make friends while I was there? Would I want to help others in need? Little by little my story about Fearless Frederic started taking shape.

I read books and old newspapers from the time (yeah, my high school French was really put to the test), and I watched films and looked up images from this incredible period in Paris's history – the *Belle Epoque*, the 'beautiful era'. I spoke to locals and visited the landmarks where Frederic's adventure was to play out.

The streets and major monuments I mention in the book are real, although I did take creative liberty with businesses like the boxing hall, horse stables and the book and toy stores. There's a little nod to *The Boy and the Spy* in there too – see if you can find it!

I had so much fun researching this book. I had to find out what police uniforms looked like back then, and what kinds of people were likely to have bought kites, and how the streets looked and sounded packed with horse-driven carts, bikes and early automobiles. I needed to do a lot of research on French desserts (yum), but I also needed to learn how the sewer system worked (ew!).

One of the things I enjoyed most about writing this story was Thierry's love of books. One of my all-time favourite stories is *The Hunchback of Notre Dame* by the legendary French author Victor Hugo. There was no way I could ignore French literature when writing a book set in Paris. France has given the world some of the greatest writers of all time, and in a very small way Thierry was my homage to them.

At the heart of this adventure is courage and friendship. Bravery isn't always about being physical. Following your heart and being true to yourself and your friends can sometimes take more courage than going into battle against an entire team of *savate* boxers.

And the things that make you different from your friends can sometimes be the very features that bind you to them. Frederic, Thierry and Claire are all very different, but somehow I get the feeling they will be friends forever. Don't you?

I hope you enjoyed reading this adventure as much as I enjoyed writing it. Maybe one day, if you haven't already, you'll get to visit Paris. Or maybe you could do your own research and write an adventure story set in this wonderful city, just like Thierry did.

I'd love to know what happens to the Floodwater Friends next or what happens to our young pick-pocket – that would be *fantastique*!

Felice

À bientôt (Until the next time!)

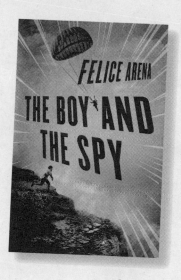

A thrilling wartime story from the bestselling author of the Specky Magee series.

Life has never been easy for Antonio, but since the war began there are German soldiers on every corner, fearsome gangsters and the fascist police everywhere, and no one ever has enough to eat. But when Antonio decides to trust a man who has literally fallen from the sky, he leaps into an adventure that will change his life and maybe even the future of Sicily . . .

Also by Felice Arena

The Boy and the Spy

The Specky Magee series
Specky Magee
Specky Magee and the Great Footy Contest
Specky Magee and the Season of Champions
Specky Magee and the Boots of Glory
Specky Magee and a Legend in the Making
Specky Magee and the Spirit of the Game
Specky Magee and the Battle of the Young Guns
Specky Magee and the Best of Oz

The Andy Roid series
The Sporty Kids series
and
Whippersnapper

Find out more at felicearena.com